Annette,

Deep Trouble

Get in
trouble :)

Annette,

but in
trouble

Also by Kimberly Kincaid

The Line series:
Love On The Line
Drawing The Line
Outside The Lines
Pushing The Line

The Pine Mountain Series:
The Sugar Cookie Sweetheart Swap, with Donna Kauffman and
Kate Angell
Turn Up The Heat
Gimme Some Sugar
Stirring Up Trouble
Fire Me Up
Just One Taste
All Wrapped Up

Rescue Squad:
Reckless
Fearless

Standalone:
Something Borrowed
Play Me

Deep Trouble
By Kimberly Kincaid

A MacKenzie Family Novella

Introduction by Liliana Hart

EVIL EYE
CONCEPTS

Deep Trouble
A MacKenzie Family Novella
Copyright 2016 Kimberly Kincaid
ISBN: 978-1-942299-37-0

Introduction copyright 2016 Liliana Hart

Published by Evil Eye Concepts, Incorporated

Author Acknowledgments

I often say that writing a book is a team effort, but it's never been more true than with this project. First and foremost, I've got to thank Liliana Hart for letting me come play in the MacKenzie world. Liz Berry, M.J. Rose, and Jillian Stein, you made the project not only a breeze, but crazy fun. To Alyssa Alexander, Tracy Brogan, and Jennifer McQuiston, for being my cheekas, I love you guys. Robin Covington, Avery Flynn, Cristin Harber, and Christopher Rice, I cannot think of more talented and or more fun people with whom to share this wild, wild ride. And to my daughters and husband, thank you for once again understanding when I jumped up from the dinner table yelling, "Wait, just let me write this idea down!"

Lastly, to my readers. I am so very excited to be starting this sexy new Station Seventeen series, and I'm thrilled to have you on the first leg of the journey with me. Buckle up, y'all! It's gonna get hot in here...

An Introduction to the MacKenzie Family World

Dear Readers,

I'm thrilled to be able to introduce the MacKenzie Family World to you. I asked five of my favorite authors to create their own characters and put them into the world you all know and love. These amazing authors revisited Surrender, Montana, and through their imagination you'll get to meet new characters, while reuniting with some of your favorites.

These stories are hot, hot, hot—exactly what you'd expect from a MacKenzie story—and it was pure pleasure for me to read each and every one of them and see my world through someone else's eyes. They definitely did the series justice, and I hope you discover five new authors to put on your auto-buy list.

Make sure you check out *Troublemaker*, a brand new, full-length MacKenzie novel written by me. And yes, you'll get to see more glimpses of Shane before his book comes out next year.

So grab a glass of wine, pour a bubble bath, and prepare to Surrender.

Love Always,

Liliana Hart

Available now!

Desire & Ice by Christopher Rice
Bullet Proof by Avery Flynn
Deep Trouble by Kimberly Kincaid
Delta Rescue by Cristin Harber
Rush by Robin Covington
Trouble Maker by Liliana Hart

Chapter One

Kylie Walker had seen a lot of bad days in her twenty-five years, some of them more foul than others. But the chest-twisting sight of two bullets being fired into her boss's head at point-blank range?

Yeah, that officially made today the most terrifying day of her life.

Kylie dropped the box of cocktail napkins in her grasp, her heart going ballistic against every last one of her ribs. Fear cemented her in front of the dry storage shelves outside the open door to The Corner Tavern's basement office, her limbs locking barely ten feet from whoever had just shot her boss as if her joints had been filled with high-powered Epoxy.

Even as her brain screamed at her to run.

Kylie's legs got the message on a five-second delay, and she spun on her boot heels. But in her desperate attempt to launch herself at the stairs leading back to the kitchen, she kicked the box of spilled napkins with a dull thump, and shit—shitshitshittyshit! She needed to get out of here before the guy with the gun saw her, or worse yet, *found* her.

Two seconds later, the rough palm on her shoulder and the cold, unforgiving press of a gun to her ribs told her she was too late.

"Let's see those hands, little girl. Nice and slow."

Kylie's breath turned to dust in her lungs as the man pulled her in from behind with a molar-rattling yank. His free hand slid from her shoulder, knotting hard enough at the base of her ponytail to make her scalp sting and her eyes water, and he pressed the gun against her body with steady, horrific pressure.

"Oh! What... I don't..." Oh God. Oh God, oh *God*. Kylie's words crashed together in her throat, tangling in razor-sharp fear. Adrenaline punched through her veins, freezing her boots to the musty concrete floor. But the man poked the gun harder against the flimsy Corner Tavern T-shirt that doubled as her work uniform, and she raised her hands to shoulder level like a puppet on sloppy strings.

"Bartender Kylie. You're quite a surprise," the man said, his voice spilling like ice water over Kylie's spine, and—wait, she knew that voice. "I thought that moron Vince had sent your pretty ass home already. Could've sworn he and I were conducting business in private."

And didn't that just make perfect sense? Her boss had closed the bar twenty minutes ago, and on a Tuesday night? They'd been dead for hours.

So to speak.

"I...I've been doing inventory in the walk-in upstairs," Kylie managed, her knees beginning to shake beneath her jeans. The surprise was mutual—she'd had no clue anyone was here other than her and Vince, and he always locked the deadbolt right at closing time.

Oh God. Vince.

"Yeah, well not anymore," the man bit out, yanking her back to the harsh glare of the here and now, and God, she wished she hadn't been so frozen in fear that she hadn't gotten a good look at him before she'd tried to run. "Now start walking toward the office. And unless you're bulletproof, I'd shut up if I were you."

Without waiting for her to comply—not that her legs were on board with anything other than going on lockdown—the guy swung Kylie away from the stairs leading back up to the bar and forced her farther into the dingy basement.

Stop. You have to be tough and make him stop. "I just...I don't want any trouble," she blurted, stabbing her feet into the floor beneath her. "I only came down here to get some cocktail napkins out of the storage pantry before I clocked out to go home."

Of course, she'd had the spectacularly bad timing of hitting up the dry storage at the exact moment the man had been putting two rapid-fire bullets into her boss's skull. Oh God, this lunatic was going to kill her. She had to stop all of this idiot shaking, get tough, and *think*.

The man's grip tightened hard enough to force a cry past Kylie's lips. "Figures I'd have to deal with the one bitch in all of bum fuck Montana who doesn't know the meaning of the words 'start walking' and 'shut up.' Maybe you need a lesson."

Kylie's heart beat so fast she grew dizzy. Pressing her lips into a hard seal, she shook her head…or at least, she tried to, but his fingers were like titanium digging into her hair.

Thank God, the man eased up a fraction at her compliance. "That's a good girl. Now get in the office so I can figure out what the fuck I'm going to do with you."

Although every last one of her hard-as-nails instincts screamed at her not to trade the narrow hallway for the deeper belly of the basement, she knew she didn't have any choice. The man clearly out-gunned and out-muscled her, and he just as clearly knew she'd seen him shoot Vince. Kylie had known when she'd taken the job that The Corner Tavern was more shady than squeaky clean and that her boss had a lot to do with the place's reputation, but he'd always been decent to her, and she needed the money. Just because he'd told her on day one to keep her eyes on the liquor and her nose out of the office didn't necessarily make him a bad guy.

Her boots clattered to a stop on the threshold of the office where Vince's body lay slumped over a growing puddle of blood, and Kylie's gag reflex kicked her in the windpipe.

"Oh Jesus." She sent up a prayer of thanks that her grabby captor had been too busy manhandling her into the room to hear the soft murmur that had barged out of her mouth. It was a small miracle that Vince had fallen on his side, his face mostly obscured from her line of sight. Of course, there were parts of him on the floor that she *could* see, parts never meant for the light of day, and she wrenched her gaze away in a last-ditch effort not to throw up at the sight of the gray matter on the floor.

"Stand right here and keep your eyes on the wall."

The man jerked her to a stop a few feet past the door, mercifully turning her away from Vince's body altogether. He released his death grip on her hair, giving Kylie the momentary rush of relief she needed to focus. She metered her breathing as best she could, searching for her older, ex-Army Ranger brother Kellan's voice in her head.

The first thing you need to do when you get jammed up is get calm and calculate.

Kylie scraped for another inhale. The guy—who she still hadn't gotten a good look at even though she was certain she recognized his voice—paced behind her, remaining silent. Although she'd only been in the office once before, she knew the only way out was the way they'd come in. Her eyes searched the grimy, dinged-up wall in front of her, mentally counting off how many steps it would take to make a break for it. But even on the snowball's chance that she'd get lucky enough to try, she couldn't outrun a bullet, and her captor had proven his trigger-happy tendencies once already tonight.

If she wanted to get out of this alive, she was going to have to disable the man first. Tall freaking order, since not only did he, *hello*, have a gun pointed at her vital bits, but she couldn't even see him to figure out his weak spots.

Not that he seemed to have any.

Growing frantic, Kylie forced herself to keep looking for something, God, *anything* that would give her an advantage, and her gaze landed on a small mirror propped up against a stack of ledgers on the filing cabinet. Vince's coke habit might not have done him any favors when he'd been alive, but his penchant for blow—or more specifically, a smooth, flat surface off of which to snort it— might just have saved Kylie's ass in the here and now.

She squinted, taking in every detail she could as the man moved into her line of sight in the glass. Recognition slammed into her as she took in the brick-end chin, the barely-there neck, the body like a Sherman tank and the flat, lifeless stare that had always reminded her of a shark, poised to go in for the kill.

Xavier Fagan. Sweet baby Jesus, the X Man was notorious for being as dirty as he was slick, getting away with every drug-related crime under the sun.

Including murder, apparently.

The jagged scar that slashed half the distance between Xavier's left temple and his stubble-covered cheek twitched as his lips bent in a sneer, and Kylie realized a beat too late that those dead, menacing eyes were locked on hers in the mirror.

"Just what the fuck do you think you're looking at?"

She clutched. There was no way she could pop off with the "nothing" on her tongue and get away with it as the truth, but emphasizing the fact that she'd been doing the polar opposite of what he'd told her to seemed like an epically stupid plan.

The second thing you need to do when shit goes sideways is find an exit strategy, came Kellan's voice in her head, and Kylie spoke without hesitation.

"I really meant what I said," she told Xavier, lasering her stare back to the wall in front of her. "All I do is tend bar. If you're here for what's in the register, go ahead and take it."

"The register." Xavier sneered as if she'd been joking, but she pressed, desperate.

"You can have all the money, the liquor, whatever you want. I don't want any trouble."

"Yeah, you look like a regular Girl Scout." The heavy soles of Xavier's boots echoed as he eliminated the space between them, the stench of sweat and something else she didn't want to contemplate pushing all the way to Kylie's lungs. Out of the corner of her eye, she caught his slow, slimy gaze as he took in her skintight jeans and the ridiculously low-cut, midriff-baring T-shirt Vince had insisted would double her tips.

Xavier reached out, the heavily inked tattoos covering his arm from shirtsleeve to wrist rippling with the flex of his muscles. Two meaty fingers hooked around the bright magenta streak in her otherwise black ponytail for another merciless yank. "So what if I take the money and run? You gonna call the cops as soon as I hit the door, Pinky?"

"N-no," she stuttered, although it was a lie. There was a huge difference between turning a blind eye to your boss's drug habit and not blowing the whistle when some thug turned the guy's brain into finger paint.

Unfortunately, Xavier saw right through her indiscretion. "Nice try, but it wouldn't matter if you did. I've got half the force in my back pocket anyway. Local, state. Fuck, I buy Feds like Christmas presents. Still…I don't leave loose ends dangling in the breeze." He stepped in toward her until the cement wall of his chest brushed her shoulder blades, his breath coming faster against the back of Kylie's neck. "But before I tie them up, maybe I'll tie *you* up."

Innuendo dripped from his words, turning her palms cold and slick, and no, no, no. This couldn't go south. She was tough. She just needed a way out, like Kellan always said.

"I won't tell anyone you were here," Kylie whispered, hating the thread of terror wobbling through the words. "I promise. I swear."

Xavier pressed his mouth against her ear, letting her feel his evil smile on her skin. "Believe me, honey. I know you won't. When I'm done with you, you won't be able to say a thing."

He ran the edge of the gun over her neck, skimming the cool steel against the spot where her shoulder met her throat before replacing it with the clammy press of his tongue. Something loosened, ugly and forceful, in Kylie's belly, and she gripped her hands into fists at her sides.

If all else fails, find the most vulnerable spot and come out swinging, kid.

Time slowed like a rubber band stretching out before her. Pure instinct had Kylie gathering all her strength in the very center of her chest, letting it collect and build and burn. With a definitive snap, her will burst upward…

And she slammed her head into Xavier's nose with all her might.

"Ah! You *bitch*." The force of the contact made him stumble back, and Kylie didn't wait to take advantage of his loosened grip. She spun around with every intention to run. But Xavier was already regrouping, his massive body coiling tighter as he hunched forward at the waist to catch the blood running down his face, and she didn't think.

Just moved.

Her foot came off the floor, connecting with Xavier's chin in a sickening crunch. His torso whipped back, hanging upright for just a split second before he fell into a heavy heap on the concrete in front of her.

Go. Go go go go go.

The command pumped through Kylie's brain, slamming against her throat with every heartbeat as she ran up the stairs two at a time. She barreled through the kitchen and into the front of the house, slowing from warp speed only long enough to put a hasty grab on the purse she'd left on top of the bar. Clutching the black leather to her chest, Kylie flung herself through The Corner Tavern's front door, not stopping until she reached the driver's side of her Mustang.

"Oh come *on*." She cursed, fumbling through the depths of her bag while keeping her eyes locked on the entrance to the bar. Relief sailed through her when finally, *finally*, her fingers closed over her key fob, her tires spitting gravel a mere ten seconds later as she tore out of the parking lot at conservatively ninety-five miles an hour.

"Okay. Okay. You're tough. You got away. You're okay," Kylie babbled, forcing herself to breathe even though each inhale was thoroughly soaked in fear.

She had to call the cops. Better yet, she had to go to the police station herself. Yeah, she'd witnessed a horrific murder—*don't think about it, don't think about it*—but if she was surrounded by cops, she'd be safe.

Kylie dumped the contents of her purse on the passenger seat, and for Chrissake, how hard was it to find one little cell phone? Mashing her foot even harder over the accelerator, she snatched up her iPhone, tapping the screen to life with a shaky jolt of her thumb.

...it wouldn't matter if you did. I've got half the force in my back pocket anyway...I buy Feds like Christmas presents...

Oh. God. Xavier might've just been talking shit. After all, he didn't strike Kylie as a trustworthy kind of guy. Then again, he *did* strike her as a dangerous-as-hell kind of guy, who dealt drugs and shot people in the face and threatened to rape and murder innocent bartenders.

Tempted as she was to call in the cavalry, one wrong step could land her in the middle of God's country with a murderer who was likely furious at having been kicked in the teeth and left bleeding all over his own crime scene.

Getting away a second time wouldn't be an option. She had to make sure Xavier didn't find her. As much as she hated admitting that she was in over her head, the stakes were too high for her not to face the hard-nosed reality staring her in the face.

She had to find someone to help her. Someone to trust with her life.

Kylie scrolled through her contacts, the white noise of her own heartbeat pressing against her ears as she pushed the *send* icon below the only number she knew by heart.

"Please…please…please answer…"

"It's four o'clock in the morning here on the East Coast, kid. This had better be a doozy."

She fought the urge to laugh, along with the even stronger urge to cry. "Kellan? It's me. I'm, uh—I'm in a little trouble. How fast can you get to Montana?"

Chapter Two

Devon Randolph rolled over in the darkness, cursing up a blue streak at his cell phone. More accurately, he was cursing whoever was on the other *end* of his cell phone, making the fucking thing ring loud enough and long enough to yank him out of the first REM sleep he'd managed to snag in weeks.

There had better be grave goddamn danger attached to this call, otherwise he was going to kick someone's ass halfway to China.

"Randolph," he grated, his mind and body both on full alert by the time he'd finished the exhale. Zero-two-thirty. SIG Sauer P229 under his pillow. Graphite-bladed KA-BAR on the night stand. Empty motel room, empty bed.

Business as usual.

"Hey, Dev. It's Walker. Sorry to wake you, but I've got a situation on my hands, and I need your help."

Devon read the seriousness between the lines of his fellow Ranger's words, digesting them in a blink. Kellan Walker was a friend, a brother. If the guy needed backup, Devon was in, no questions asked.

"You straight at the fire house?" he asked. Kellan had

channeled his adrenaline into fighting fires after they'd gotten out of the Army three years ago. Funny, really, that Devon put out fires, too—just that the heat he dealt with while freelancing private security jobs was a lot more figurative than literal.

"Yeah. This is actually a family thing. Not about me. Well, not directly, anyway."

Devon took in the intel, keeping his surprise to himself. "Copy that. What's going on?"

"Please tell me you're still out there in BFE." Kellan's voice stretched thin, barely covering the words.

"I'm crashing in Montana, not outer Mongolia," Devon said for the sake of clarity. After all, he and Kellan had done no less than a dozen ops in places more remote than Surrender, Montana, and Devon couldn't help it that his sister Cat had ended up marrying the town doc here. There were worse corners of the world to kill time between jobs with MacKenzie Security, and he and Kellan had been to most of them. "But if that's what you mean, then yeah, I'm still in the zip code."

His buddy exhaled a hard breath. "Thank fucking God. You remember my sister Kylie, right?"

"Yeah. Of course." Probably five years had passed since Devon had met her when he'd hung with Kellan on R and R, but between her smart mouth and her tough-girl demeanor, Kylie would be difficult to forget. Especially since she and her brother were tight, to boot.

"I just got a phone call from her. She's been working at some dive bar in Grant's Pass for the last six months."

Devon's mind spun in calculated thought. "I passed through the town on my way here a few weeks ago. It's about an hour from Surrender." Not much to write home about, if he remembered right. And he always did.

"Well, that puts you a hell of a lot closer than me." Kellan paused. "She's jammed up pretty bad, Dev."

Shit. "How bad?"

"Bad enough to call me and ask for help for the first time in our lives. She witnessed a local drug dealer by the name of Xavier Fagan murder her boss, and then the guy came after her."

"Jesus," Devon breathed. "Where is she now?"

"Safe," Kellan said, and didn't *that* explain why the guy hadn't gone completely over the edge in the re-telling. "She managed to get away from Fagan, but she says the guy is no joke. Apparently he's really well connected, all the way up to the Feds."

On second thought, "shit" wasn't even in the same hemisphere as this. "So she can't call the cops."

Kellan murmured an affirmative, followed by a couple of nasty curse words. "Exactly. I got her about fifty miles from Grant's Pass, and she's safe for now, but the first flight out of North Carolina doesn't leave until oh-seven-forty my time."

"Which won't put you in BFE until nightfall." Commercial flight across the country was a bitch and a half. The drive from the airport to Surrender? Even worse. "So how do you want to run this?"

Kellan paused, his normally unshakeable demeanor sounding like someone had taken a whack at it with a tire iron. "Do you think you can sit on her and just make sure she's okay 'til I can get there tonight? Kylie's tough, and I've got her holed up pretty tight off the grid…"

Devon frowned, running a hand over his dark blond high and tight. "But?"

"But she's my kid sister, and you're the nearest resident badass," Kellan said. "Fagan sounds like a nasty son of a bitch. I'd feel better knowing you've got eyes on her until I can get there."

"Then I guess I'd better get eyes on her ASAP." Devon tossed the sheet off his hips, skinning into the pair of jeans he'd left on top of his duffel at the foot of the bed.

"Thanks, man." Relief marked his buddy's words, but Devon didn't even break stride in the search for his bruised and battered work boots. Everything he did, he did full throttle. Plus, he owed Kellan, and not a little.

And since Devon's biggest fuck-up had nearly cost both their lives, the least he could do was get his ass out of bed and prove his worth by looking after the guy's little sister.

"No sweat," Devon said, covering his shrug first with a white T-shirt, then his shoulder holster. Hell, he had a sister, too. As tough as Kellan's might be, Devon got the guy's need to look out for his family. "I'm awake, and you need backup. What's Kylie's location?"

Kellan released a slow breath over the phone line. "She stopped at the El Monaco Motel about an hour outside of Grant's Pass, room 202. She's driving a red Mustang with California plates. I told her not to open the door for anyone, no matter what."

Easy enough. "I'll head out there, see what I can see."

"Thanks, man. I really appreciate it."

"You give her a code word so she'll know I'm a friendly?" The last thing Devon needed was to have Kylie panic—or worse yet, run—in a case of mistaken identity.

"I wasn't sure if I'd get you, but tell her you're there to deliver the jelly donuts. That's my code word, so she'll know you're solid."

Under different circumstances, Devon would be tempted to give his buddy a ration of shit over his choice of code words. But they had a job to do, someone to protect, so this shit would have to wait. "Copy that."

"Her cell reception's pretty crappy, but I'll try her back to let her know you're coming. And Dev?"

"Yeah?" he asked, switching to his Bluetooth device so he could use both hands on the job they were meant for.

"Do me a favor and watch your six, would you?" Kellan asked. "On the off chance Fagan gets lucky enough to find her, he won't hesitate to hurt her. Or worse."

For the first time in ages, Devon let loose with a smile, triple checking the clip in his SIG before turning to get his backup nine millimeter from its hidey hole under the bathroom sink.

"Trust me, Walker. I'm on my toes. Your sister will be safe with me 'til you get here. I swear it."

* * * *

The El Monaco Motel turned out to be twenty rooms of stop and fuck about a mile off the highway. After doing a drive-by to give himself a mental map of his surroundings, Devon parked his year-old Dodge Challenger around the back of the place, sinking low in his leather jacket as he walked the perimeter. The motel was a good thirty minutes closer to Surrender than Grant's Pass, but then again, distance was different all the way out here. The open stretches of land, the way the remote plains and uninhabited landscape unfurled on an endless loop, reminded Devon of a less dusty version of Afghanistan.

If you move, I will kill your friend.

"Knock it off," he muttered, shaking himself back to the here and now. Stepping so his shit-kickers remained silent on the cracked pavement, he scanned the space in front of him from left to right. Two-story motel, ten rooms up top, ten ground level. Points of entry open to either an outdoor walkway or the front parking lot itself. Six vehicles in the lot beneath the blue neon sign boasting rooms for the night or by the hour, three pickup trucks, a newer-looking SUV, a rust-encrusted Toyota…

And what do you know? A red Mustang with California plates.

"Hmmm." Devon moved toward the vehicle, his eyes taking a quick tour of the empty interior. He flattened his palm on the hood, swinging his gaze up to the door marked 202 in cheap, reflective numbers.

The car was still warm. Kylie was here, but she hadn't been for long.

"Don't fucking move."

The purposely roughed-up voice came from behind, accompanied by a steely nudge that told Devon he had his work cut out for him. Goddamn it, now he was going to have to break someone's kneecaps before the sun even came up.

Bright side was, at least he'd get a workout.

"All right," Devon said, lifting his hands to feign submission. "Take it easy. I'm just looking for a friend."

"A friend." The voice dripped with sarcasm, but there was something weird about the disguised tone, something Devon couldn't quite place. The figure came into view in the reflection of the windshield for just a split second, but it was all he needed to gain the advantage. Spinning around, he wound his arm over the guy's above the elbow, capturing both his arm and his weapon in one decisive move as he pulled the guy forward…

And realized he wasn't a guy at all.

"Ow! Oh my God, get off of me." The woman's chest, which was now all sorts of up close and personal with Devon's, expanded with a brewing scream, and he reached out to clap his free palm over her mouth before she woke the dead.

"Kylie?"

Her wild stare widened, unnaturally blue beneath the neon and moonlight, but she didn't stop struggling.

Jesus *Christ*. "Kylie, hey, take it easy. Your brother sent me. He—"

Searing pain shot through his middle finger, and he whipped his hand back from her mouth as a low oath launched past his own. "Did you just bite me?"

The venomous look on her face answered his question, lickety split. "My brother didn't tell me he was sending anybody."

Damn it, Kellan must not have been able to reach her after he and Devon had gotten off the phone. "Cell service is for shit out here. He called me forty minutes ago, right after he got off the phone with you. I guess he couldn't get you again."

"And you just happened to be in the area? I don't buy it. Who sent you?"

Devon's brows shot upward. "You do realize that I'm holding *you*, right?" He squeezed the arm he had on lockdown, not hard enough to hurt her, but with enough pressure to punctuate the message.

"I can still scream," Kylie said, her breasts lifting against the stupid-low neckline of her T-shirt.

His hand—which was bleeding, for fuck's sake—clapped back over her mouth in an instant. "If I wanted to hurt you, I'd have done it six times by now. So do you want to do me a favor and let me help you like I promised Kellan I would? He said he sent me to deliver the jelly donuts."

At the sound of her brother's name and the code word he'd clearly given her, she stilled, her dark brows drawing in tight. "How do you know my brother?" she asked as soon as he lifted his fingers again.

"We were in the Army together. Afghanistan. Uruzgan

Province. He's a hell of a sniper." It was an understatement, but the details worked to keep her from screaming her head off. "I actually met you five years ago in San Fran."

Half their team had done that R and R together, and they'd only spent one night of that around Kylie, throwing back beers at the local bar where she'd worked. It was a last-ditch to expect she'd remember him.

Even though Devon sure as hell remembered *her*.

"Wait…" Kylie's eyes took a tour of his face, narrowing to near slits before springing wide. "Devon? Holy shit, is that you?"

He eased his hold on her at the same time her muscles loosened beneath his grasp. "Yeah. It's me."

"Oh my God, I didn't even recognize you. You look…" She straightened, clapping her mouth shut instead of finishing her sentence. Not that Devon couldn't fill in the blanks.

He knew damn well how much harder around the edges he'd grown since the last time he'd seen her. Just like he knew damn well what had caused the change.

Kylie wrapped her arms around herself, taking a step back on the pavement. "When is Kellan coming?"

"It's going to take him at least half a day to get out this far. Until then, I promised to keep an eye on you."

"I don't need any help," she said, hiking her chin despite the waver in her voice, and yeah. Whatever paces Fagan had put her through tonight were clearly bad enough to come with an adrenaline letdown. Still, Devon needed to keep her safe, and that wasn't going to happen if she went around trying to be all Brenda Badass in dark parking lots.

"Uh huh. You've obviously cornered the market on assaulting people with—" He paused just long enough to spare a glance at the weapon he'd heard fall to the ground when he'd grabbed her, and seriously? This shit was too good to make up. "A Maglite."

"It was all I had in my car," Kylie groused. "Anyway, you're lucky it's the smaller version, or I'd have cracked you over the head with it."

Guess she had a point there. "Do you want to tell me why you're jumping people in the parking lot of the No-Tell Motel at three a.m.?" Devon asked, releasing her arm and taking a step back to look at her.

"First of all, I didn't *jump* you. Secondly, you're the one who was poking around my car."

Kylie bent down to scoop up the discarded flashlight, stuffing it into her oversized purse and knotting her arms over her chest as she pushed back to standing. A swath of dark hair had fallen loose from the disheveled ponytail at her crown, cloaking her eyes in shadow. Her high cheekbones and lush, sassy mouth were on fully display though, and as Devon slid his gaze lower to take in her skimpy T-shirt, the flat slope of bare skin between the red cotton and the top of her jeans, and her legs that went on for days, he swallowed hard in realization.

Kylie might be Kellan's little sister, but she was one hundred percent grown woman.

"Okay, fine," Devon said, blanking the heat in his veins before it reached his cock. Yeah, Kylie was fucking gorgeous, but she was still off-limits, not to mention in danger. "That still doesn't tell me why you're not locked inside your room like you should be."

"I…I haven't eaten since lunch, and I was starting to get the shakes. Kellan's always harping about how adrenaline screws with your blood sugar, and I knew I wouldn't be any good if I passed out. I was on my way to the gas station over there because it's close. But then I saw you messing with my car, and…well, you know the rest."

Smart girl. Right up 'til that last part, anyway. "Taking a potshot at a guy you don't know when you're at a tactical disadvantage isn't a very good move."

"Thanks, Captain Obvious. I get that now."

Kylie dropped her chin, squeezing her baby blues shut despite her fiery comeback, and aw, hell. She'd obviously been through the wringer tonight. No sense in dragging that out.

"Okay, look. Let's get you something to eat. Then you can grab some sleep and when your brother gets here tomorrow, we'll get everything to stand up straight, all right?"

"O-okay," she said, backpedaling as she added, "Thank you. You know, for coming out here while I wait."

"No problem." He tried on a smile to put her at ease, realizing a beat too late that she'd return the favor, and fuuuuuuuck, as tentative as it was, her smile was still a stunner.

Devon nodded, forcing his shit-kickers toward the spotty fluorescents lighting up the gas station half a block away. Christ, he was an asshole of the highest order to think about Kylie's smile even for a second. He busied himself with surveying the area, but the darkest part of night in the middle of Montana didn't really offer much by way of riveting shit.

They made it to the Gas and Go without any fanfare, Devon sticking close enough to Kylie's side to keep her safe while still giving her enough breathing room to keep her calm. He added a large bottle of water to the bag of pretzels she'd plucked from the shelf, giving the clerk a tight smile and a ten spot to cover the bill.

"You need to stay hydrated," Devon said, handing over the water as they recrossed the threshold to the parking lot. Kylie's lashes fanned up in surprise, but she cracked the bottle open for a couple of healthy swigs without argument. For the first time since he'd stumbled upon her, Devon noticed the shadows beneath her eyes, the lines of worry etched over her pretty face.

"So do you want to talk about what's going on here?" Devon asked, although he damn near regretted the question before it was all the way out. She'd witnessed something nobody should ever have to see. She'd probably give her left arm to forget the images that must be burned into her brain.

Just as he opened his mouth for a full retraction, Kylie said, "I guess telling you what's going on would help, right?"

"It might." At least, that's what all the shrinks had told him after his debacle in Afghanistan. Not that he'd taken that little nugget to heart. "But only if you want to."

Kylie bit her lip, her boots beating out a steady crunch-crunch-crunch against the roadside gravel. "I, uh—I was at work tonight and something...really bad went down."

Even though Kellan had briefed him on the phone, Devon didn't interrupt, only nodded. Better to let her tell the whole thing if she was looking to unload some stress.

"I'm a bartender at this place called The Corner Tavern. Or I guess I was, because…" She clutched the bag between her fingers hard enough to make it crinkle. "I…I…my boss always said to keep my nose out of the basement, especially the office, but we ran out of cocktail napkins, and he's such a pain in the ass when I don't restock everything before I leave, and I knew I wasn't supposed to, but…"

"Kylie." Devon's bad-things meter kicked up a notch, but she barreled on, either not noticing his attempt to keep her grounded or not caring.

"I just went down there for a second, you know? For one stupid box of napkins. I must have been in the walk-in when Xavier came in. I didn't have a clue he was even in the bar until…until…" Her voice bottomed out to a thin whisper as she finished. "Until he shot my boss in the head. Twice."

Although Devon hated his next question, he had to be sure. "And you saw the whole thing happen—you didn't just hear it or see your boss after the fact?"

Kylie's head moved up and down, her dark hair swishing against her shoulders as they crossed back into the motel's parking lot. "I, uh…yeah. I saw the shooting happen, and then Fagan tried to kill me, but I got away, so…"

Devon's blood turned subarctic in his veins. More questions swarmed his brain, but truly, his number one priority was to hustle Kylie inside so they could wait for Kellan in safety before she said another syllable.

He scanned the parking lot. Three pickups. Two SUVs. The rusted-out Toyota. Kylie's Mustang. No people. "Okay. Let's go up to the room and get you out of sight. Then—"

Devon stopped short.

Two SUVs. Not one.

"We need to move." He slung an arm around the slim line of Kylie's shoulders, leaning in to drop the words in her ear. "Slow and easy, Kylie." His hand found his SIG in exactly that fashion, fingers closing around the butt of the gun as he steered her toward the back of the motel.

"But I thought you said…oh my God." Her entire frame went bowstring tight, her head whipping toward the SUV. "The guy getting out of that Escalade. That's him. That's *him*."

Yup. Time to freaking get gone. "My car is behind the motel. Don't look back. Just go."

Kylie turned the corner, her breath hitching with audible relief. "I see it. I think we can get there in time."

They were four paces from freedom when the first shot whizzed past Devon's ear.

Chapter Three

The sharp edges of fear that Kylie had just managed to smooth into submission burst back through her at warp speed. Her boots slapped the pavement, her body unable to move fast enough to obey the primal demand pumping down from her brain

Run.

The running lights on the sleek black muscle car in front of her glowed a dusky gold, the engine growling to life as she hurtled closer. A loud pop-pop-pop registered in her ears, the sound not making any sense until she saw Devon swing around with a gun in his hand to fire off a round, then two in return.

Oh my God, they were going to die.

"We're not going to die," Devon said, making Kylie realize she'd spoken the words out loud. "Just get in the car and keep your head down."

He didn't have to tell her twice. She yanked the door handle hard enough to make her fingers smart, throwing herself into the passenger side of the car and curling her arms over her head. Devon was right beside her, jamming the key in place to keep the remote-start circuit running as he threw the car into gear and tore out of the back lot.

"Are we safe?" Confusion filtered past the slam of Kylie's heartbeat. She poked her head up in an effort to at least try to see what was going on, but Devon's steely stare pinned her into place, mid-move.

"No." He leaned into the accelerator even harder, making the engine roar. "Stay down. And put your seatbelt on."

Three tries later, she finally got the stupid thing clicked into place over her chest. "I'm sorry. I did everything Kellan said. I don't know how he found me—"

"Whoever this Fagan guy is, he's not here for amateur night. When you started working at this bar, you filled out paperwork, right?"

"Yeah," Kylie said. "Job application, tax stuff…" Oh God. "And a copy of my driver's license."

Devon cursed under his breath, as if he didn't want her to hear it. "Then chances are he's got a lock on your identity. Do you have any local family? A boyfriend? Roommate? Anyone?"

Her head shook, along with the rest of her. "No."

"Good." He blew past the on-ramp to the highway, making a rough turn down a narrow side street. Although Devon's stare was lasered in on the rearview mirror, he maneuvered the car forward with ease, finally pulling into a makeshift parking lot behind a scrap metal yard. He backed into a spot by a rickety shed, scanning their surroundings one last time before killing both the lights and the engine.

"We're going to *stop*?" Kylie's jaw fell open. She sat upright to protest some more, but Devon's hand landed on her shoulder, keeping her scrunched down in the passenger seat.

"We got a pretty decent jump on Fagan, although I have no doubt he tried to follow us." Devon unbuckled his seat belt, methodically checking the clip on the big black gun he'd had in his grasp ever since they'd taken the holy shit route out of the motel parking lot. "Chances are he'll assume we hit the highway to outrun him."

"And we didn't why, exactly?" Outrunning that maniac sounded freaking fantastic to her.

"Because that's what he thinks we'll do. Probably," he tacked on.

"Probably," Kylie repeated, her heart pounding so hard surely Devon could feel it where his fingers still splayed over her shoulder and neck.

He shifted his weight against the driver's seat, swiveling his gaze through the shadows being cast by the lone dingy bulb at the opposite end of the scrap yard. "You told your brother Fagan has connections with some bad police. Did you call nine-one-one tonight? Even for a second?"

"Oh." Kylie blinked, trying like hell to keep her mind on the question and not the fact that they might get discovered, shot, and left for dead. In that order. "Um, Xavier bragged that he has half the police force in his back pocket, all the way up to the Feds. I was scared that if I called nine-one-one, he'd know where I was, so no. I didn't even try."

Devon tipped his head in a nonverbal *smart move*. "If Fagan's got cops on his payroll, it explains how he found us. He probably pulled your registration from the DMV database. After that, it was just a matter of looking for places you might hide."

Kylie cursed her stupidity for staying put. "I knew I should've kept driving." Her pulse picked up the pace, and she cut a glance in the direction of the road beside them. Not that she could see anything other than the shadow-lined interior of Devon's car with how she was slumped way down in her seat. "Don't you think he'll find us again? I mean, we're only what? Five miles from the motel?"

Devon lifted a shoulder, his leather jacket shushing in the dark. "We just have to lie low and wait to find out. Speaking of which, slide down lower in your seat so you're completely out of sight. You can move it back a little farther if you need room for your legs."

She did what he asked even though logic warred with her instinct to trust him. "Correct me if I'm wrong, but doesn't this make us sitting ducks?"

"No. It makes us tactically smart. Fagan is probably tearing up the highway right now with his hair on fire trying to find us in a place that we're not. We have a clear path to the on-ramp as an exit strategy on the off chance he didn't bite. I know I can outrun that Escalade he's in." Devon flicked a glance through the windshield at the hood of the muscle car. "But I don't want to unless I have to."

"Oh." *Way to offer up the lamest response in the galaxy.* Devon's plan made sense, she guessed. At least, it would have if sitting still wasn't going to give her the mother of all panic attacks.

Kylie swallowed hard, forcing herself to focus on something that wasn't the possibility of Fagan finding them in short order. Her eyes landed on Devon, and she took a minute to really check him out.

He looked so different than the quiet, easy-to-smile guy she remembered, to the point that she hadn't recognized him in the parking lot. Now that her vision had adjusted to the scant light and the shadows in the car, she could make out his harder features in detail—the sharp blade of his nose, strong cheekbones, firm mouth. His hair was dark blond, but really, that was half a guess since it was short enough to make her unsure. Although he'd lifted his hand from her shoulder in order to take a low, defensive position in the driver's seat, Devon was still within less than arm's reach, his body coiled with controlled tension.

Oh, his body. Even through his jeans and leather jacket, Kylie had been able to discern that he was bigger and more imposing than he'd been five years ago, one hundred percent muscle. Hell, he'd been pressed against her hard enough in the parking lot to prove it. But Devon wasn't just bulk, clumsy force with no follow-through. His body was dangerous and graceful all at once, as if he was spring-loaded, just waiting to unleash that intensity onto something. Someone.

Jeez, it was hell-hot in this car.

"Devon, I—"

"Shh!" His demeanor changed in an instant. A ripple in the shadows on the dashboard at eye level told Kylie headlights had appeared at the top of the side road leading back to the highway, and oh God. She knew—she *knew* Xavier was too smart and too mean not to find them.

"Devon. Oh my God, what do we do?" Panic lanced through her chest, spreading out to seize all four of her limbs in less than a breath.

With a lightning-fast turn of his wrist, Devon had his weapon at the ready, his frame dropping low across the front seat. The move flattened his back across her chest and belly, and even though his legs remained on the driver's side of the car, considering the size of his six-foot-plus frame? He couldn't be comfortable draped halfway over her.

"Shh. Easy." The sound arrived on less than a whisper, Devon's whiskey-brown eyes flashing up to hers as the headlights drew closer. He gripped his gun with his right hand, holding it carefully at his side, but no way could they just sit here and wait to get blasted.

"Devon." She pushed the word out as calmly as possible, but his body tensed all the same. His free hand lifted to her mouth, his forefinger and middle finger applying just enough pressure to keep her from adding to the convo. Kylie noticed then that he'd moved so his mouth was only inches from hers, his breath slow and warm between them, and she scraped for an inhale despite the cold shards of fear spiking all the way through her.

We're not going to die. Devon's voice echoed in her head. His stare pierced the changing shadows, calculating, watching, taking in every shift and nuance. The headlights approached at a steady pace, ratcheting Kylie's heartbeat faster and faster as the interior of the car grew brighter.

Devon's fingers curled against her lips just a fraction harder as if to say, steady…steady…

And then the car passed by without any fanfare, not even braking as it continued down the side street and off into the dead of the Montana night.

"Kylie. It's okay. We're safe."

Her breath escaped in a dizzying whoosh. Afraid that if she opened her mouth to respond, she'd do something stupid like start to cry, Kylie simply nodded, but holy crap, she wasn't going to be able to keep it together much longer.

Her boss was dead. Murdered. Fagan was after her; he knew who she was. He wasn't going to stop until he found her, and when he did, he was going to——

"Kylie, look at me."

Under any other circumstances, she'd probably have bristled at being bossed around. But somewhere between the blood and the bullets and the bad guy, everything had hurtled out of her control, and God, why couldn't she *breathe*?

"I…I…"

Nope. No go. Her chest squeezed, constricting as if all the air had been sucked out of the car and replaced with liquid cement. A tremble worked its way up from her very center, and the ripple effect made her shiver and sweat at the same time. Devon's fingers slid from where they'd been resting over her lips, hooking gently in her hair as he put his face directly in her line of vision.

"Hey. Hey." His whisper was soft, so unlike the one that had come before to quiet her and so *very* unlike his rock-hard demeanor that Kylie blinked, her panic slipping just an inch.

"There we go, yeah," Devon murmured. "Look at me." His thumb found the spot on her jaw just below her ear, smoothing a slow circle over the skin there, and the movement snagged enough of her attention to keep her shaking in check. Sort of.

Devon leaned in, his chest covering hers in strong, steady warmth. "Whoever was in that car was just passing by, okay? See— no lights. No sounds. Nothing out of the ordinary. It wasn't our guy."

Kylie's heartbeat continued to slam, the white noise whoosh of her blood pressing hard against her eardrums despite her desire to be tough. "F-Fagan could still be coming. He could still find us."

"He could. But we wouldn't be sitting here for a second if I thought he *would.*"

This time, Kylie's blink was one of slow realization. "So...are we safe? Can we get out of here now?" Please, God, she just needed to get out of here, out of this car and this state and this whole situation.

"I think we're okay," Devon said, although he didn't let go of her. "But I want to give it a few more minutes, just to be on the safe side."

Her throat knotted. "Devon, I can't. Please, I need to—"

"Breathe," he finished, and funny how her lungs got on board with that quiet, commanding voice. "I need you calm, Kylie. I need you with me."

With him. Right. She could do this. She *could.* "Mmkay," she murmured, although she still wasn't convinced she was anywhere close to okay.

Which must have made two of them, because Devon didn't

budge. "What's your favorite thing to eat for dinner?"

"What?"

The question was so ridiculously out of place, but still, he didn't take it back. "Mine's chicken Parm, although it's tough to go wrong with a good, old-fashioned New York strip."

"Um." Kylie took a breath and thought for a second. "I guess mine is spaghetti and meatballs." Her stomach let out a rumble at the thought, and wasn't that just embarrassing, considering her midsection was less than a foot from Devon's ear right now.

"That's a good one," he said. "S'pose you'd have a nice bottle of red with that, huh?"

"Maybe." Her muscles let go a little against her seat, and she leaned into the heat of Devon's palm, still firm and strong and sweet against her cheek. "Yeah. Pinot noir. Or, no, Chianti. That would be perfect."

"So here's what I want you to do. Every time you get scared, I want you to close your eyes." He paused long enough for her to let her eyes flutter shut for a trial run, but then his words continued, low and hypnotic. "Good. Like that. Then I want you to picture that dinner."

Kylie's laugh was as soft as it was involuntary. "Really?"

"Yes, really," Devon said, his smile hanging just slightly in his voice. "Red and white tablecloth, garlic bread, the whole nine. You got it?"

She nodded, her shoulders going lax. "Yes."

"Okay. Now every time you get scared, or you think something bad might happen, I want you to grab onto this picture in your head. Because once we get you safe, you're going to have that dinner."

"Do you promise?"

Somewhere, in the logical part of her brain, Kylie knew Devon couldn't promise she'd be okay any more than he could promise her the moon on a pie plate. But between the quick, calculating actions he'd taken to get her away from Fagan and the slow, soothing circles his thumb was tracing over her jaw, she couldn't deny the truth.

If Devon said yes, she'd believe him.

"Yes. I promise, Kylie."

Something about the way he said her name made her open her eyes, recognizing all at once how his body pressed against hers, his chest to her chest, his mouth not even an inch away. Heat roared through Kylie's belly, quickly turning to slick wetness in her panties, and even though it was insane, she lifted her chin to close the space between them. Devon exhaled against her mouth, but whether it was shock or something deeper, Kylie couldn't be sure. Want like she'd never, ever felt flared to life in her blood, driving her to search, to take.

And she did.

Kylie reached out, wrapping her arms around the muscle-covered expanse of Devon's shoulders. The leather from his jacket created just enough friction on her bare forearms to turn her want into a demand, and she didn't hold back. Devon's fingers flexed at the hinge of her jaw, his mouth resting on hers with just the barest brush of contact before he pressed against her harder with a groan.

Oh God. Yes. Yes. Kylie swept her tongue over the seam of his lips in a bid for more, and all at once, he gave it. His mouth parted, but not to let her in. No, Devon's lips slanted over hers with the clear intent to take, and he kissed her hard, desperate. Wild heat built between her legs, her pussy clenching with need beneath the damp satin of her panties. Digging her fingers into his hard, leather-clad shoulders, Kylie matched the intensity of the kiss, even as it grew along with her want. She moaned, parting her mouth, her thighs, her *everything* so Devon could kiss her, touch her, take her more fully.

But then she realized he'd stopped kissing her back.

Devon grated out a low curse, pushing himself back to the driver's seat in one fluid motion. "Kylie. We can't...I need to keep you safe."

She blinked, her cheeks burning even though the rest of her chilled from the sudden non-contact of their bodies. "Oh! I, uh. I'm sorry, I didn't mean to—"

"No. This is on me. Adrenaline can do crazy things. You're not used to that, but I should've known better. It's my *job* to know better."

"I'm here too, you know." Kylie pushed herself to sitting, her moxie slowly coming back online. "It takes two to tango, and all that." Kissing him might've been impulsive, but she wasn't about to deny having wanted it.

"Still. I was way out of line," he said, his unshakeable demeanor falling right back into place as he swept the parking lot with one last glance before hitting the car's automatic ignition button. "We've waited long enough to be safe for now, but we need to get moving now that you're calmer."

Kylie's gut sank to her boots. Of course he'd just been trying to calm her out of her panic-induced tizzy, nothing more. God, had she seriously been so jacked up on adrenaline that she'd tried to devour him like an all-you-can-eat buffet? She must be out of her freaking mind, not to mention a few other parts. "Right. Sure."

He eased the car out of the gravel lot, doing the exact speed limit as he re-traced their path over the access road. But once again, Devon skipped the pleasantries of the highway, opting instead to turn onto a two-lane state route that—by the look of things—was a hell of a lot less traveled.

"Where are we going?" she asked, and the unyielding set of his jaw sent the tension winging right back into her shoulders.

"We're going to get out of the immediate area, then find a place to rest and recon for a few hours. I need to get a plan into place."

"A plan for what?"

Devon didn't hesitate. "For keeping your brother off that plane."

Okay, she couldn't possibly be hearing right. "What? Why?"

"Because if this guy knows enough about you to track you through the DMV, then by now, he knows who Kellan is, too."

The thought of Fagan going after her brother turned Kylie's stomach into a corkscrew. Still… "If anyone can take care of himself, it's Kellan."

"I know." Devon's gaze hardened as he lasered it through the windshield and into the predawn. "But if Kellan gets on that plane, he'll lead this asshole to you like a homing beacon. We've got to take Plan B."

Already, she hated the sound of this, but no way was she going to stay in the dark. "And Plan B is?"

"First, we're going to figure out how to run the murder you witnessed up the right chain of command so we can take Fagan down. But you're right—if we stay too long in one place, he has a better chance of finding us."

"Okay," Kylie said, trying like mad to process the thoughts flinging themselves around in her already overstuffed brain. "So what does that mean, exactly?"

Devon turned, his copper-colored stare as fierce as it was determined. "It means Kellan's going to figure out how to get you into protective custody, and then we're going to nail this guy to the wall. In the meantime, since your brother can't come to you, I'm going to take you to your brother. One state at a time."

Chapter Four

Devon stared at the highway, the dull gray ribbon of asphalt stretching as far as he could see. The darkness had faded a few hours ago, and Kylie right along with it, both seemingly out of the energy required to continue.

His hard-on, however, had picked up the slack in spades.

As if she could see him through her zzzzzs, he cut a quick glance at Kylie in the passenger seat, adjusting his dick to a less socially awkward position while mentally singing "99 Bottles of Knock It Off, Asshole." She was in a metric fuckton of danger, not to mention being Kellan's sister. The same sister the guy had flipped his goddamn lid over when Devon had called to brief him a couple hours ago on their run-in with Fagan. The same sister Devon had sworn to drive two thousand miles to safety.

The same sister he'd coaxed out of a panic attack by way of putting his tongue in her sweet, sexy mouth, and fuck, he really was a degenerate of the highest order.

Double fuck, a deep, dark part of him had wanted to do so much more than kiss her.

"Ugh." Kylie stirred slowly from her spot next to him, her blue eyes doing the open and close routine as she adjusted to the land of the living.

"Morning," Devon said, sending one last *not for you* to his cock before sliding a glance in her direction. Christ, even with bleary eyes and bedhead, she was still sexy as hell.

"It's still morning?"

Devon nodded, and yeah, this was good. They should stick to the basics. "Just shy of oh-nine-hundred. How'd you sleep?"

"Like I'm running for my life," Kylie said, wincing as soon as the words were out. "Sorry. I get kind of sarcastic when I'm scared. Kellan says it's a defensive thing. But you didn't sleep at all, so I shouldn't complain."

"You also shouldn't apologize." Devon lifted a shoulder halfway, then let it drop back into place against the black and red leather of the Challenger's driver seat. "Ingrained defense mechanisms are a good thing. They mean you're a fighter." Annnnd since he wasn't going to get a better segue, he added, "Now that you're up, we should talk some specifics."

Her body tensed, but he had to give her credit. Her chin stayed nice and high. "Okay."

"We're just outside of Billings right now. That puts us roughly thirty hours from North Carolina." Devon had mapped the route with Kellan during their phone conversation, and it hadn't been all chuckles.

"Why do I sense the word 'but' coming on?" Kylie asked, and man, she got right to it.

Not that he minded. "*But* we have to stick to some less traveled routes, and we definitely can't go tearing across the country like there's a Molotov cocktail strapped to our asses. If we get pulled over, we go right into the system. Even if the cop who writes the ticket isn't dirty, chances are, if Fagan is the player he's claiming to be, he'll still find it."

Devon didn't want to add—out loud, anyway—that the guy almost certainly had whatever network was at his disposal busting its ass to try and find the Challenger, and if he'd managed even a partial ID of Devon's plates during all the duck and run last night? That could send shit FUBAR in a heartbeat or less.

Kylie shivered even though the sun was already promising to warm the June day well into the eighties according to the radio's weather report. "Did Kellan have any ideas on who to take this to?"

"He's got a few contacts he trusts at the NCPD, but it's going to take a little time. We don't want Fagan to know we're sniffing around," Devon said. "The more we stay under the radar, the better. At least for now."

"So until then, you and I just road trip to North Carolina?"

"'Fraid so." Devon knew it was probably the last thing she'd ever wanted to do. "By the time we get there, Kellan should have a safe plan in place. I keep a go bag in my trunk, so I've got a decent amount of cash and a few changes of clothes." And a veritable arsenal, complete with plenty of ammo, but that pretty much fell under the umbrella of well, duh. "We'll have to stop and get a few things for you. I mean, uh. You know. Under...garments and stuff."

Kylie nodded, turning about the same shade as the magenta streak in her ponytail, which brought him to Point B. "We're going to need to cover up your hair, too, unless you want to cut it."

"You're not serious." She pinned him with a look that suggested he'd gone around the bend, her hands flying up to the now-loose elastic keeping her hair (sort of) in check.

"The pink is pretty conspicuous. All I'm saying is that changing it would make it harder to spot you. But covering it is an okay alternative."

She sat back in her seat, pressing her lips together for a full minute before reaching for her purse to start rummaging through its contents. "Well, it's not much, but I got decent tips over the weekend, so I have a hundred and fifty-two dollars in cash. I also have my phone, the Maglite, some toiletries..." She trailed off, her brows sliding together as she looked at him. "What?"

He let out an exhale loaded with remorse. "About your phone. I'm gonna need it."

"But I turned it off when we left the motel, just like you asked," Kylie said. She held the thing up as proof, and man, Devon felt like shit for what he was about to do.

Not that he wasn't still going to do it. "I know, but there's still a chance it can be tracked. It would take a lot of time and effort, so the chance is small, but it's not worth the risk."

"So what are you going to do with it?"

"Truth?"

She nodded, and he wished like fuck she hadn't because now he had to say, "I'm going to pull over in the next secluded spot I see and put a couple nine millimeter slugs in it, just to be sure the GPS won't out our location."

Her breath escaped in a shocked chirp. "You're going to *shoot* my phone?"

"Sorry. But yeah."

"What about yours? If Fagan knows your car, he knows you. Can't he track your phone too?" Kylie challenged, knotting her arms over her chest. Goddamn it, they were going to need to find her a new top when they stopped for supplies. Preferably one with the dimensions and sex appeal of a burlap sack.

"No," Devon said, pulling over on a sandy shoulder on the desolate stretch of road. It was as good a spot as any, and the sooner he got rid of her technology, the better, really.

"*No?* That's all you've got?"

Damn, she hadn't been messing around when she'd warned him about the sarcastic/defensive thing. "First of all, we don't know that Fagan can ID my car. But secondly, I freelance private security for a living. When I'm on the job, my personal cell goes under lock and key in a safe location. After that, it's strictly burner phones, so I tossed the one I was using after I briefed your brother."

Kylie's dark brows shot upward. "You tossed it. As in…?"

"Out the window, about a hundred and ten miles ago. I already swapped it for a new one, just in case."

"Oh." She bit her lip, her eyes darting out the window as he slowed the car and pulled over to the shoulder. "I guess you've thought of everything."

That, and he owed her brother the crown jewel of debts for the one time he *hadn't* thought of everything and had ended up endangering not only himself, but his entire team, including Kellan. Not that Devon wanted to go there right now—or, okay, ever. "This is my job, Kylie. I keep people safe."

As if to prove the point, he nodded at the cluster of trees just past the shoulder of the road where they'd stopped.

"You want me to go with you while you blow my phone to kingdom come?" she asked.

Devon answered her question by getting out of the Challenger and rounding the front of the vehicle to open the passenger door for her. "Your brother trusts me to keep you safe, which means you don't leave my sight unless absolutely necessary."

For a second, she looked like she might argue. But something shifted in her bright blue stare, prompting her to murmur, "Whatever blows your skirt up, I guess."

He led her through the trees, just enough for them to have cover while still keeping one eye on the car. Dropping her phone in a bald patch in the grass, Devon paced off about fifteen steps, because seriously, shrapnel was a bitch best left alone.

He unholstered his backup weapon from its spot just above his left ankle. "Go ahead and get behind me. And you're going to want to cover your ears."

Although she looked way less than thrilled about it, Kylie did as he asked. She stood close enough for him to feel her flinch at both shots he fired into her iPhone, but he had to hand it to her. Rather than get uppity about the ruined tech or complain about lost contacts the way some people did, she simply waited for him to make sure the GPS had been effectively disabled.

Two seconds later, the deed was done, and twenty more had them back in the Challenger, driving away from the blasted bits that used to be Kylie's cell phone. Devon refocused on the road, figuring he had another hour, maybe two before they'd have to stop for gas, food, and a little shuteye.

"So private security. That must keep you pretty busy," Kylie said, and he steeled himself against the curiosity glinting in her eyes. The last thing he needed was to get personal with her, despite the stupid what's-your-favorite-dinner crap he'd pulled earlier.

"Uh huh."

She waited out the silence for a minute, then two. "Have you been out of the Army for three years like Kellan?"

"Mmm hmm."

Another pause, but still, she didn't let up. "And you've been doing security the whole time?"

"Yup."

Kylie arched a dark brow, turning to peg him with a high-level, no-bullshit stare. "Are you going to be this chatty the whole time we're stuck together? Because really, all these details are wearing me right out."

Whether it was her sassy mouth or his adrenaline finally letting down after being shot at a handful of hours ago, Devon couldn't be sure. But his words launched out before he could tamp down the urge to give them air time.

"I'm thirty-one years old, and I've lived pretty much all over the map. I went into the Army right after high school, because it was either that or follow in my old man's footsteps as a career criminal. Became a Ranger three years later, took a few strolls through Iraq and Afghanistan, and now I'm back here stateside, freelancing security gigs, most of them with a private company run by my brother-in-law's family. Were there any other details you wanted, or did I hit the highlights for you?"

Her wide-eyed expression combined with her stunned silence to punch holes in Devon's gut, and Jesus Christ, he was an *ass*.

And he hadn't even let loose the part where he'd foolishly let himself get taken hostage on an ambush, not to mention how her brother had risked his life to save Devon's about three nanoseconds before some scumbag insurgent buried a bullet in both of their gray matter.

Devon opened his mouth for a sloppy retraction, but Kylie beat him to the one-two. "No, that's pretty good, actually."

"What about you?" he asked, even as his better judgment howled at him to stand down and shut up. But at least talking about her would be better than opening his yap about the not-so-good old days.

"Me? I'm pretty much an open book, I guess. Kellan and I don't have much by way of family, but he's six years older than me, so he does the protective thing a lot."

Devon's brows climbed upward. "You're only twenty-five?"

Kellan had never mentioned the age gap between him and Kylie, and she was tenacious enough that Devon never would've guessed it was more than a year or two.

"Yeah, but I've been pretty much on my own since Kellan went into the Army. After high school, I did a semester at community college, took some cooking classes." She shrugged, although the rise and fall of her shoulders was just a little too stiff to carry genuine nonchalance. "I like to cook, but jobs in the front of the house are easier to get, so I just bounced around waiting tables and tending bar. That kind of thing."

"Why stick to waiting tables if what you really want is to be in the kitchen?" It was a flyer, but Kylie's chin lifted ever so slightly, and bingo. Devon hit pay dirt.

"Money, mostly. I never had enough to go to culinary school," she murmured, although her tone said that whatever made up the rest of the reason was responsible for the tension suddenly triple-knotting her muscles against the passenger seat. "Anyway, that's why I left California last year. I had a bad breakup, lost my job. I wasn't going to find another one if I stuck around, not to mention having nothing to stick around for. So I headed as far east as I could until I ran out of cash, and that's how I ended up in Montana."

Devon's head buzzed with so many questions that choosing one to put to words was a tall order. "California's huge. Losing your job sucks, but how is it that you couldn't find another one nearby?" There had to be hundreds of restaurant gigs, even in Cali's smaller cities and towns.

Kylie laughed, although there was zero humor in the soft huff of her breath. "Let's just say when you're a better cook than your 'chef' boyfriend"—she paused to pin the word with an air quote/eye roll combo—"and your interview for the open kitchen position at the café where you both work puts that fact on display? Egos get bruised like summer fruit."

"That explains the breakup." Well, that and the fact that her ex sounded like a gold star member of the Dickhead of the Month club. "But if you were a better cook, how come you didn't get the job?" Devon asked.

"Because my ex was better in the bedroom than the kitchen. He seduced the restaurant manager and convinced her I was power hungry and that I'd be a tyrant in the kitchen. She fired me, and restaurant circles are more like rumor mills. My resume was pretty much Swiss cheese at that point anyway, so…"

"You took off." Something else she'd said tugged at the back of Devon's mind, and before he could haul the question back, he asked, "You said you got as far as Montana. Where were you headed?"

Kylie paused, although her expression remained tough. "I haven't been to the East Coast in a while. I thought it might be cool to go see Kellan."

"See him? Or live in NC?"

"Whichever," she said, but the word came out with way less indifference than he'd bet she intended to stick to it.

"Why didn't you tell your brother you wanted to move to North Carolina?" Hell, he'd bet Kellan would've moved a mountain range to bring Kylie closer to him if he'd known that was what she wanted. Devon would do the same for his own sister Cat in a nanosecond.

"Because I'm a big girl," she said, just as matter-of-factly as if she were telling him she had blue eyes or that the earth was round and not flat as a two-by-four. "I was stuck in California of my own doing, and that's exactly how I was going to get out. I might move around a bunch, and sometimes I fly by the seat of my pants, but I can still take care of myself." Her gaze shot out the window as she tacked on, "Most of the time, anyway."

Devon opened his mouth to tell her she didn't have to be so tough. The last thing either of them needed was for her to pull another stunt like the Maglite stickup she'd tried last night in the motel parking lot, and just because Kylie was fierce didn't mean she was bulletproof. But then she turned to grab her sunglasses out of her purse, and the look on her face slapped him right in the solar plexus.

She might rather stick a pin in her eye than admit it, but she was barely hanging on. Which meant they needed to stop and get some supplies and shuteye ASAP.

Because not only had Devon been in those exact same shoes four years ago, but if he didn't regroup and get his shit together, he was liable to do something galacticly stupid.

Like tell Kylie he knew just how she felt.

Chapter Five

Kylie split her gaze between the navy blue baseball hat in her lap and the mom-and-pop drugstore to her right, unsure which one she liked less. The hat Devon had pulled out of his glove box was sure to be an obvious cover-up, and that was *if* she could actually cram all her hair under the thing. Then again, the store was a fixed place, an unknown place, and despite the cheerily painted sign and the trio of wide, sparkling windows gracing the front, Kylie knew all too well that the worst sort of bad might still be lurking inside.

"We're going to be fine," Devon said, sliding his gun into the holster beneath his rib cage before covering it seamlessly with his leather jacket. "Just keep your eyes open and try to relax, okay?"

She bit back the joyless laugh welling in her throat. "Tropical beaches are relaxing, Devon. This"—she paused to flick her wrist at the storefront—"is my own monogrammed version of hell."

"I get it," he said, and funny, he actually looked like he did. "I know the whole situation is intense. But the more at ease you look, the less likely we are to attract attention. From anyone."

Kylie twisted her hair behind her nape, awkwardly wrangling the baseball hat over the thick knot and adjusting the brim. "Then how come we didn't go to the Walmart a couple exits back?" It had been the first and only sign of major civilization since they'd hit the road. "Wouldn't blending in there have been easier?"

"Maybe. But a more crowded place has a lot of moving parts that are hard to control, not to mention security feeds we'd be sure to show up on. Getting in and out of a place like this will take us ten minutes, tops, with a whole lot less visibility to boot."

She followed his lead and got out of the car, sending covert glances around the nearly empty parking lot. Despite Devon's powerful presence barely two feet from her dance space and the fact that he probably had enough weaponry on him to protect a small nation, Kylie's heart still took up residence in her windpipe. Sweat beaded beneath the ill-fitting baseball hat, her palms growing clammy enough to slip off the handle of the drugstore's front door.

"Everything's fine," Devon murmured, so close to her ear that his breath tickled her neck. "Just remember your spaghetti dinner, okay?"

She nodded, forcing herself to try on a shaky smile. "With wine."

"Now we're talkin'."

He opened the door just as easy as you please to usher her inside, and okay. Okay, yeah, this wasn't so bad. At least as far as running for your life went, anyway.

Kylie picked up a plastic basket, looping the handles over her arm. Scanning the store's aisles, she was relieved to see the place sparsely populated at best, and definitely not with anyone who looked remotely frightening.

She released the breath that had been spackled to her lungs. "I only need a few things."

"Okay," Devon said. Although his stare traveled over every inch of the store, he kept to the whole white-on-rice routine as she walked down the first aisle, her skin prickling with awareness at how closely he shadowed her every move.

"Don't you need to get some things too?" she asked, sliding a toothbrush and a travel-sized tube of toothpaste from the shelf.

"One or two."

Kylie waited out the dozen or so heartbeats of silence between them before finally sending a pointed look down the aisle. "Did you want to go do that while I finish up?"

"I'll wait."

He rocked back on the heels of his boots to look at her like nothing doing, and something inside her chest snapped. Kylie wasn't stupid—she got how dangerous her situation was right now, and how much worse it could be. But the aisles were low enough to make the entire store visible, and the whole place was four, maybe five rows, max. She didn't want to run free, but she did want to get the hell out of there as fast as humanly possible. Other than a young woman with a baby on her hip and the store clerk, who was eighty if he was a day, the store was empty; plus, she wasn't completely soft. Was a handful of paces to choose her deodorant really too much to ask when the place was obviously safe and sound?

Kylie dropped her voice to a whisper, tucking back a strand of hair that had escaped the lopsided perch of her hat. "You said you need to keep eyes on me, right?"

"Kylie—"

"It's fifteen feet, Devon. And it'll cut our time in half."

He swiveled a gaze around the store, a muscle tightening over the smooth angle of his jawline. "We're leaving in two minutes. Don't dawdle."

His footsteps sounded off against the faded linoleum as he moved to the next aisle. Even though he was still in Kylie's direct line of sight, the space let her breathe. She grabbed some toiletries, pausing for only a second in the hair care section before aiming herself at the rack of clothing by the far wall. The selection was pretty sparse—just a handful of touristy T-shirts and some basic supplies, but she managed to score a package of utilitarian cotton panties and some men's tank top undershirts, along with a hoodie.

On her way back to Devon, Kylie plucked a king-sized Snickers bar from the end cap display, tossing it on top of the supplies in her basket. After witnessing a murder, being chased by a vicious criminal, and watching her cell phone get blown into a billion sky-high pieces, really, she deserved a little slice of indulgence. Especially since Xavier Fagan was still out there, and Kylie had no doubt he'd do whatever was necessary to hunt her down and put a bullet in her skull for what she'd seen.

On second thought, she'd earned a hell of a lot more than a candy bar, even if Snickers *was* her favorite. Like a nice long bubble bath, with an hour-long massage on top.

Add a couple of sheet-ripping orgasms to the list, and you've got yourself a party, sweetheart.

"Did you find everything you needed?" Devon asked, appearing from the other side of the brightly colored candy display, and Kylie nearly blushed herself into spontaneous combustion.

"Uh huh," she managed to choke out, holding up the basket and following him to the register. One blond brow went up as he caught sight of the Snickers bar, but Devon remained thankfully quiet as they paid for their items and headed back to the car.

"There's a motel around the corner. Looks like a good place to get some rest."

"Okay." Kylie pulled off the baseball hat, what little hair that had remained in place spilling sloppily over her shoulders. She might feel too wired to close her eyes, and the shot of sexy impulse that had just unexpectedly popped her in the sternum hadn't helped to calm her, but still. A nice, hot shower and a place to stay hidden sounded like heaven right now.

Except that she had to go into yet another public place in order to get them, and God, would this stupid panic ever ease up?

"Don't worry. This will only take a minute," Devon said, and the gruff reassurance sent a prickle of heat over her cheeks.

"That obvious, huh?"

His lifted shoulder was answer enough. "You did fine in the store. Chances are, snagging a room will be even easier."

"I don't suppose I can talk you into letting me stay in the car while you run inside." It was a long shot, Kylie knew. But for some reason, the car felt safe. Secure.

Devon's eyes flashed, amber-brown and full of *no*. "It's my job to protect you. That means you go where I go. No exceptions."

He skimmed a glance through the windshield to take in the small roadside motel, and even though she had no idea what she was looking for, Kylie did the same. The place looked like a direct relation to the El Monaco, right down to the hourly rates and the mismatched letters on the VACANCY sign. While that might squick her out under normal circumstances, right now, staying at a place without cameras rolling or questions asked did seem pretty smart.

Kylie stuffed her hair back under the baseball hat and followed Devon out of the car. A fresh hit of adrenaline tightened her chest like a steel band, threatening to swallow her right there on the pavement.

But then he turned to look at her, his expression steady and sure. "Just a walk in the park. I promise," he said.

You've got this, girl. Devon's got this.

They walked the dozen or so steps to the motel's front entrance, Kylie's nerves growing looser with each step. Devon brushed a hand over the small of her back as he ushered her over the threshold, and even though the motel's lobby was as dated and dingy as she'd expected, she managed to squeak in a semi-deep breath.

"Help you?" asked the man behind the counter, although he'd barely looked up from the poorly concealed *Hustler* propped open over the desk.

"We need a room."

Devon's voice carried enough gravel to grab the man's attention, his bleary eyes going wide at the sight of Devon's imposing stance less than two feet away.

"Oh! Uh, right. So I just need your ID and a credit card," the man said, the stink of stale cigarettes and fresh gin punching her in the nose from across the counter as he stood.

"I'll pay cash."

"I'm not supposed to…" The man trailed off, his gaze narrowing first on Devon, then on Kylie, lingering on her skimpy T-shirt for two seconds too long. "Oh, I get it." His greasy grin grew into a leer. "Don't want the wife to catch you, huh?"

A muscle flexed in Devon's jaw. "Something like that," he said through his teeth.

"Whatever you say, boss. I don't judge. But for that kind of upgrade, there are service fees."

Kylie put a stranglehold on her urge to knock the guy's block off, mostly because she and Devon got what they wanted. Devon slipped the manager some extra incentive to work both quickly and quietly to turn over the key to a room on the ground floor, and ten minutes later, they shut (and locked and chained) the door behind them.

Devon closed the drapes, doing a quick sweep of the dated but surprisingly clean room before slinging his duffel bag over the bed closest to the window. "Go ahead and lie down if you want to," he said, shouldering out of first his jacket, then his holster. "I'm sure you're beat."

"I'm fine," came her auto-reply, but the words were as close to a lie as they'd ever been. Kylie blinked, the surreal memory of the last day and the steady presence of his gun making her pulse beat harder in her veins. "Actually, I'm going to take a shower. I kind of really want to get out of these clothes."

"Oh." His throat worked over a swallow, his gaze dropping to his duffel bag. "Right. I have an extra pair of sweats if you want them while we crash. Not ideal, but——"

"Sounds great. Thank you."

Her voice hitched even though she fought to keep it steady, the ensuing silence making her weakness sound that much more obvious in her ears. Mashing down on the mix of emotions suddenly churning through her belly, she grabbed the sweatpants Devon had pulled from his duffel and the two plastic bags from the drugstore, hightailing it into the bathroom before he could ask if she was okay.

Right now, she was a lot of things. Shaky. Mad. Scared. Amped up.

But at the moment, "okay" was definitely not on the list.

She upended the bag with the toiletries into the bathroom sink, forcing herself to get everything in order. The task calmed her, and she started the shower, turning back to open the oblong box she'd chosen from the hair care aisle. Kylie pulled off the horrible skimpy bar T-shirt she never wanted to see again, then her boots and jeans, every movement methodical, each motion a tiny success.

She was tough. She could do this.

She could survive.

Lather, rinse, repeat had never been so ironic. Kylie stuck to the tasks in her head—*scrub your hair, shave your legs, rinse your skin*—until finally, she stepped out of the shower. One last unopened package gleamed up at her from the sink, but even though her chest ached at the sight of it, she took a deep breath and looked at her reflection in the steam-misted mirror.

"Fuck it."

Chapter Six

Devon set up his weapons just as he did in every motel room he stayed in, with his SIG within arm's reach and his KABAR in the nightstand, and a variety of other mean-and-nasties strategically placed throughout the small space. His phone had been silent since he'd activated it a handful of hours ago, and he reached out to palm the thing, tapping in Kellan's number from memory.

"Tell me you two are holed up someplace safe," his buddy said, and oooookay, so much for pleasantries.

Which was cool, because Devon wasn't exactly a tea and crumpets kind of guy. "Copy. You got anything on this douche bag yet?"

Kellan's pause spoke of nothing even remotely good. "Xavier Fagan, also known as the X Man, is on no less than a dozen wanted lists from Montana to Mississippi. Priors for possession with the intent to distribute, weapons, and he's been ID'ed as the main player in a heroin ring the size of Yankee Stadium."

"And he's still on the street how?" No way a guy who was in it that deep wasn't at the top of the FBI's dance card.

"Because he's not blowing smoke about being well connected," Kellan said. "Fagan seems to have a gift for sniffing out bad police, the higher up the food chain, the better, and he's old school. Does all his business face to face, and all his dirty work himself. Word on the street is that he even murdered his own brother because he thought the guy was ratting him out to the cops."

Devon sank into the timeworn chair across from the foot of his bed. "So the Feds who aren't in his pocket want him, they just can't make anything stick because their witnesses always end up in body bags." Fucking fantastic. "You turn up anything by way of assistance from your contact at the NCPD?"

"The rundown I just gave you is courtesy of her," Kellan said, his voice shifting slightly enough that if Devon didn't have noticing every last detail branded into his DNA, he'd have missed it.

Interesting. Devon filed that little nugget away to pursue when his personal safety wasn't twisting in the wind. "She have any higher-ups you can trust? I can keep Kylie safe for a while, Walker, but the longer we play cat and mouse, the harder it's gonna get. We need an end game here."

"Detective Moreno works in intelligence, and she's a good cop. But getting jurisdiction is easier said than done. She's on it, though. Hard."

Devon had no doubt that Kellan would be a four-foot thorn in the woman's side until she came up with a solution. "Copy. For now, I'll keep moving toward your location."

"Thanks," Kellan said, pulling in an audible breath over the phone line. "I really owe you, Dev."

"You owe me nothing, Walker. I'll check back in at twenty-one-hundred your time. Call me if you get anything from Moreno."

Devon disconnected the call, scrubbing a hand over his jaw. Although he knew Kellan would have both hands full getting the X's and O's into place to get Fagan snatched up, Devon wasn't concerned about whether or not his buddy would make that happen.

What *did* worry him was that Kylie had now been in the bathroom for forty-five minutes, and despite the fact that there were no windows in the tiny room and he could hear her moving around, Devon had a bone-deep feeling she was far from all systems go.

He pushed himself out of the creaky bedside chair. While he wasn't exactly Mr. Congeniality, or even a nice guy for that matter, she'd been through a shit-slide of emotions in the last day. A quick hey-how-are-ya couldn't hurt.

But before Devon could make it halfway across the carpet, the bathroom door pushed open, and Kylie stepped silently over the threshold.

"Hey. I was just coming to—"

Devon's words tripped to a halt in his throat. Kylie stood barely three steps away, wearing a thin white tank top and his borrowed sweatpants that she'd had to roll over her hips twice to even get them close to staying up. But her unconventional apparel wasn't what had frozen him into place from lips to legs.

"You cut your hair," he finally managed, and Christ, nobody would ever accuse him of being suave. But come on. She'd gone into the bathroom with a long, hot pink and black ponytail and now she was sporting a head full of chin-length, caramel colored hair that looked just tousled enough to be hot as fuck.

"Yeah, I…" Kylie broke off, taking a steady breath that outlined the press of her breasts against her tank top. "You were right. The pink was really obvious. I knew hiding it wasn't going to work in the long run, and anyway, it's just hair. So I cut it."

"It looks…" *Do not say wildly sexy, do not say wildly sexy, do not say…* "You know. Pretty."

Kylie's laugh rode out on a soft puff of humorless breath, and man, she was a fighter. "I don't know about all that, but I guess it's not terrible. There were a few pieces in the back I couldn't reach, though."

She extended the scissors in her hand just far enough to hammer home her request, and Devon's chin snapped up in shock.

"You want me to cut the rest of your hair?"

"Well, yeah. It'll be pretty obvious if I leave it like this, won't it?" she asked, gesturing to the handful of thick strands still cascading down her back.

Damn, she had a point. Still… "Cutting your hair is a little outside my wheelhouse, is all."

Okay, so the words were a massive fucking understatement. Devon could dismantle an AR-15 with one hand chained to a radiator, but cutting Kylie's hair?

Unless she handed over a pair of clippers and asked for a standard issue crew cut, he didn't have clue one what to do.

But Kylie just served him with a no-nonsense stare. "This whole thing is outside my wheelhouse, Devon. But I trust you with my life. My hair is kind of the least of our worries, don't you think?"

"You trust me with your life." The words echoed in Devon's ears as he repeated them, and her brows tugged downward.

"Of course. I mean, I'm here with you right now, hiding from Fagan."

"Oh. Yeah, sure." He took the scissors from her, suddenly needing something to focus on other than her wide-open honesty. Of course Devon had known she trusted him to a point. Her brother had sent him to keep her safe, and she damn well needed protecting—both truths that Kylie clearly couldn't ignore. But trusting him because she was in over her head was a whole lot different than trusting him instinctively, and he only needed a glimpse at her bright blue stare to know that she meant what she'd said in spades.

Kylie trusted him without question. Just as her brother had in Afghanistan.

When he shouldn't have.

Hot, dust-choked air…sweat running down his back beneath his gear…turning to give Kellan the all clear…

If you move, I will kill your friend.

Devon cleared his throat, although the gesture did nothing to ease the tightness log-jamming his vocal cords. Sliding his thumb and forefinger through the scissor loops, he waited for Kylie to turn around before threading his opposite hand through her hair. She smelled sweet and clean, like flowers and fresh bedsheets, and even though he didn't need to, Devon ran his fingers all the way to the ends of her hair twice, because that's the sort of bastard he was.

To his total surprise, Kylie melted into his touch.

"Thank you," she said, her voice notched down to a throaty whisper that made his dick stir behind the fly of his jeans.

Christ, he needed to concentrate. He angled the scissors over a strand of her hair, opening and closing them in a precise cut. "For what?"

"For coming to the motel when Kellan called you. For keeping me from getting killed. For staying so calm when I'm not. Take your pick."

Devon was tempted to tell her all of that was part of the job, that he owed her brother a thousand favors that would get him shot at and chased across the country. That he wasn't calm so much as he simply hadn't allowed himself to feel anything for the last four years.

But instead, he stuck with a gruff "You're welcome," making another cut with the scissors, then a few more still before adding, "You know, not staying calm in situations like these doesn't mean you're not tough. In fact, all that emotion is a good sign you're normal."

Kylie's shoulders tightened slightly, although her chin stayed on the level. "Yeah. I'm sure the pure-terror panic is really helpful in keeping me safe."

"It's normal," Devon reiterated. "Plus, you're doing just fine. I've seen guys twice your size cry for their mommies at the slightest whiff of danger."

"Really?"

"Really." He moved around to Kylie's side, reaching for the last long lock of uncut hair. His fingers accidentally brushed the bare skin on her shoulder, just above the strap of her tank top, and damn, how could she be so soft when he was so loaded with rough edges?

She turned her chin, looking up at him from over her shoulder. "Are all the emotions normal? Even the ones caused by the adrenaline, like you said?"

The glint in her eyes did nothing to make his cock stand down, and Devon swallowed hard. Kylie was off-limits. Forbidden. Way too good for a guy like him.

Also, quite possibly the most gorgeous woman he'd even seen in his life, who was currently looking at him with unmistakable hunger he wanted nothing more than to sate, again and again and again.

"Kylie." Fuck, even her name was like sin in his mouth. "What you're feeling right now is—"

"Want," she said, the flush on her face looking as if it had damn little to do with being bashful. "I don't care if it's the adrenaline making me feel this way. The truth is, today could be the last day I've got."

"It's not."

Although Devon met her stare with equal intensity, trying like hell to fight the heat tearing through his veins, Kylie still turned all the way around.

"I want you anyway, Devon. Right now. Without regrets."

His heart slammed, his restraint waning fast. "We can't."

"We can," she whispered, her lips so close he could feel the hypnotic heat in her words. "All you have to do is say yes."

Kylie's curves were the perfect contrast to the hard angles of his body, pressing against him in all the places he ached to be touched and licked and fucked, and in that split second of dark, greedy want, Devon knew he'd love every second of giving her what she'd asked for.

Even if he hated himself for it later.

He slanted his mouth over hers in a kiss so bruising and hot, he could taste the desire on her tongue. Kylie matched his need measure for measure, opening to let him in while taking back at the same time, searching and stroking with her lips, her tongue, her teeth.

"Oh, God." Kylie's words collapsed on a moan, and Devon's pulse ramped higher in his chest as she tipped her head back to give him better access to her neck.

The heat in the lowest part of his belly became an outright demand. "You need to be sure," he bit out, grabbing for the last thread of his already unraveling composure.

She didn't hesitate for a second. "I've been sure since I kissed you last night."

It was all Devon needed to hear. He loosened his grip on the scissors, tossing them far enough away to keep from being caught underfoot as he maneuvered Kylie backward to the bed. Splaying one palm wide over the paper-thin cotton covering her shoulder blades, he lowered her to the mattress, dividing the frame of her body with his hips.

Good Christ, he wanted to rip every last stitch of clothing from her body and push his cock into her, hard and fast and five seconds ago. But as much as the basest part of his brain urged him to do exactly that, the fierce, needful expression shaping Kylie's features made him pause.

He might not be worthy of her outside this room, but he knew how to make her feel alive. For just a little while, Devon could keep her safe and help her forget. He could give her what she needed.

And he meant to do it.

Right now.

Forcing himself to slower movements, he angled over Kylie's body, bracketing her shoulders with both hands. For a second, all Devon did was take her in—the scant light from the bathroom creating gold-tipped shadows across the lines of her throat and collarbone, the soft cotton pressing against her chest as it pressed against his hammering heartbeat in turn. Years had passed, four of them, to be exact, since he'd taken his time with a woman.

But just because he was taking his time with Kylie didn't mean he'd make her wait to come.

Shifting his body to one side, Devon surrendered his weight to the mattress while keeping one denim-covered leg between the heat of Kylie's thighs.

"Look at you." He skimmed a hand from her shoulder to her hip, letting his gaze follow the path. Her stare dropped to his fingers, the shock of her acquiescence making his balls go tight with realization.

Watching turned her on.

Making certain she had a perfect line of sight to both his hands and his mouth, he slid his palms over the flat of her belly, reaching for the hem of Kylie's shirt to tug the cotton over her head. She'd foregone a bra, making Devon send up a fervent prayer of thanks, even as he let out a soft swear at the sight of her breasts.

"Jesus, Kylie." He slid a thumb over one berry-colored nipple, his mouth starting to water as it tightened further under his ministrations. "You're goddamn perfect."

Kylie wrapped her legs around his thigh, thrusting hard even though her eyes stayed focused on the hand cupped firmly beneath her breast. "Devon, please."

Her throaty whisper raked over him like a touch, and he answered her request without words. Devon parted his lips over her nipple, sucking the beaded peak all the way into his mouth, working her in time to her thrusts against his thigh. Pulling back just slightly, he eased his thumb past his lips, alternating soft swirls of his tongue with rougher-edged touches from his hand.

"Oh. Oh God, don't *stop*."

Kylie arched upward, her spine bowing up from the cool, white bedspread to fit more of her against his mouth. Devon slid his attention to her other breast, licking, sucking, daring her closer to the edge until her hips pistoned against him. Unable to hold back, he yanked the rest of her clothes from her body, wedging his jeans-clad leg back between her thighs.

"Look," he grated, the heat of her pussy driving him insane even through the layer of denim between them. "Look how fucking hot you are. How wet. How sexy."

Kylie's eyes drifted from his mouth to the spot where his body rubbed mercilessly against her bare sex. The friction had left a damp spot at the top of Devon's thigh, and he slid over her again, this time harder. Her stare darkened with building need, turning almost midnight blue in the dim light of the room, and it loosened something low and powerful in his chest. Keeping a steady rhythm between her legs, he returned his focus to her breasts, rolling one nipple between his fingers while slipping the other greedily back into his mouth.

"*Oh.*" The high sound emerged from the back of her throat, turning Devon's cock to solid steel, but rather than making him falter, her honeyed moans had him picking up the pace.

"That's it, baby. I've got you. Come undone for me."

Kylie's body went still and tight, motionless for just an instant before she began to tremble beneath his hands and mouth. He rode her through every gasp and every lust-blown breath, only dialing back his touch when her body finally went loose against the mattress.

"You're a little overdressed for the occasion, don't you think?" Kylie finally asked, her pointed glance still on the spot where her naked body came together with his clothed one.

An odd sensation Devon couldn't quite name turned over in his gut. "We don't have to do this," he said, but she simply pinned him with that sassy stare that made him want her all the more.

"Let me ask you something." She slid from beneath his body, kneeling against the comforter as she pulled him up to face her. Her hands dipped beneath the hem of his T-shirt, exploring the bare skin beneath it, and fuck, he couldn't *think* when she did that.

"Okay," he managed, helpless against Kylie's touch. Holy hell, there went his T-shirt.

She licked her lips, kiss-swollen and flawless. "Do I strike you as the sort of person who does things without wanting to?"

"No." His answer flew out, as unchecked as it was honest.

"Good. Because I'm not. I might be impulsive." Kylie ran her fingers down the plane of his chest, her mouth curling into a wicked smile at the jump of his muscles when she went lower, then lower still. "But when I said I wanted this, I meant all of it."

She freed the top button on his jeans with a quick turn of her wrist, and Devon was lost. Kylie felt too damned good to refuse, with her hands making quick work of his clothes and her lips hot at his ear. Hooking her fingers into the waistband of his dark gray boxer briefs, she lowered the cotton until his cock sprang free.

"Ah." Devon's breath burst from his lungs on a sharp exhale, but it didn't stop Kylie from circling her fingers around him in a slow, sinful glide. Her hand rode his cock with just enough suggestion to make him crazy, squeezing from base to tip. His pulse beat a wild pattern against his throat as she teased. Stroked. Pumped. But the sensation was too much and not enough at the same time, and finally he pulled back with a curse.

"I want to be inside you, Kylie." As if to illustrate his point, Devon reached out, dusting a finger up her leg until he reached the sweet, slick spot at the junction of her thighs. She pressed her knees into the now-rumpled comforter and canted her hips into Devon's touch as he slipped his finger inside the tight warmth of her pussy.

Kylie's moan of approval twined around his. "Give me a second," she said, sliding from the bed to the bathroom. His confusion turned to relief when she returned a few heartbeats later with a condom between her fingers.

"I might be impulsive," she said, tearing open the packet and putting the condom on him with only a few easy touches. "But I'm not stupid. I keep them in my purse."

Devon made a mental note to sing the praises of preparedness later. After they'd exhausted both themselves and her entire stash of condoms. "Come here."

She pressed against him in reply, unabashedly naked. He gripped her waist, his hands wide and rough on her skin, and he laid her back on the mattress. Kylie parted her legs, knotting her arms around his rib cage to pull him close. The head of his cock brushed her sex, the wet heat sending a bolt of raw want sailing all the way through him, and Devon was done resisting. He thrust into her body, driving deep in one hard stroke.

And then he lost his mind. Or maybe he found it, because truly, he'd never wanted to hold onto something so badly in his life.

A moan slipped past Kylie's parted lips. "Oh, *God*, Devon."

Her inner muscles squeezed around his cock, her hips beginning to move in a deliberate glide, and he was powerless to do anything but meet it. He pulled away, just slightly, before thrusting back between her legs, the sweet pressure of her pussy gripping him tight as she stretched to take him completely. But the want was too dark, the need too urgent, and within seconds, he'd foregone every slow, sensual thing he knew Kylie deserved in favor of fucking her, hard and fast and deep.

But she was no wallflower. Kylie met every thrust with a moan, digging her fingers into his shoulders, fucking him back even faster. She was gorgeous and wild, her tawny hair tangled over her face, pale skin covered with the sexy sheen of her exertion as they pounded together over and again. Her core was so tight, so hot and slick around the heavy hardness of his cock that his control flickered, threatening to short out.

Devon knelt between her legs, flattening his palms over the silk of her inner thighs to spread her wide. Kylie's stare glittered between them, landing on the spot where his cock slid into her sex-slicked pussy, and he gave in to the dark, deep urge to make her come. Without breaking the rhythm of their hips, Devon moved one hand from her thigh, burying his thumb in her folds just above where they joined.

Her nails curved into his wrists, the sting all pleasure. "Don't stop," she begged, her hips jerking upward to chase the movement of his fingers on her clit. "Please, just…"

The rest broke from Kylie's throat on a cry. Her back arched, her body bowstring tight with the power of her climax as she came apart beneath him.

"That's it, baby. Jesus, you're so beautiful," Devon whispered, covering her body with his to let the words fall over her skin and into her hair. He kissed her, searching for God only knew what, and a moment later, she began to move again. Dark pleasure uncurled at the base of Devon's spine, and he moved with her, thrust for thrust. Kylie dropped her hands to the comforter, curling the fabric in tight fists and locking her ankles around his hips to hold him deep inside.

Too close. Too perfect. Too much. He anchored his hands beside her on the mattress, pumping relentlessly as his orgasm razored up from his balls, the release so strong that it bordered on pain. Filling her to the hilt, his breath turned into her name, tumbling past his lips over and over as he came hard enough to see stars.

For a minute, an hour—fuck, it could've been a month—there was nothing but him and Kylie. Then Devon filtered back to the motel room, detail by detail, bit by bit. After a quick trip to the bathroom to deal with the condom, he returned to the bed, the reality of what they'd done, what *he'd* done, already spinning up in his mind.

But Kylie just pulled back the covers, reaching out to him with a warm, lazy smile, and his unease became something else entirely.

"We're safe here, right?" she asked. "For a couple of hours?"

"Yeah." Even though he knew he shouldn't, he slid into the bed next to her and wrapped her in his arms. "I've got you, Kylie. You're safe. I swear."

Devon had never meant anything more. Even if he had to die to prove it.

Chapter Seven

Kylie slipped the last of her toiletries into her purse, giving her reflection one final look in the smudgy glass over the bathroom sink. The drastic change in her appearance still felt surreal, as if she were looking into a trick mirror that spit back someone else's image entirely.

Although between the life and death danger she'd endured last night, the impromptu hair hack, and the undeniable post-sex glow lighting up every corner of her face, the concept of Kylie being a totally different person than yesterday really wasn't much of a stretch.

"You almost ready?"

Devon's voice was quiet and serious, just as he'd been since they'd woken up from their power nap twenty minutes ago. Between their pair of fast showers and the couple of protein bars they'd thrown back while packing up the room, she and Devon hadn't had much of a chance to exchange more conversation than was necessary. But even though sleeping with him had been impulsive, Kylie had no regrets, and she'd be damned if she'd let him crawl back into that rough, gruff shell of his just because she was his buddy's little sister and they'd had some really hot, really consensual sex.

Holy mother of God, the sex had been incendiary.

"Yeah. Listen, Devon." She paused to follow him over the threshold and into the main room, the sight of the rumpled bedsheets sending a bloom of involuntary heat between her legs. "Before we go, I just want to make sure we're good."

His shoulders tightened just a fraction beneath the black cotton of his T-shirt, but the look on his face betrayed nothing. "Of course. I'll do whatever's necessary to keep you safe."

"I know," Kylie said, her answer both automatic and truthful. "That's not what I mean, though. I want to make sure we're good. Me and you."

For a minute, then two, Devon stood completely quiet in front of her. But then he surprised the hell out of her with, "I owe your brother a lot, Kylie. I wanted this"—he broke off to meet her stare, gesturing between them with one hand—"I want it still. But there's more to it than me and you."

"There isn't." Kylie's heart squeezed, but she closed the space between them with certainty. "Right now, this is *only* me and you."

He opened his mouth—to argue if his hard-edged expression was any indication—but she cupped her hands around his face, cutting him off before he could start.

"Look, I don't have a crystal ball. I don't know what will happen between us, and I get that you and Kellan are close. But that doesn't mean I don't want this in the here and now. So what do you say we just keep moving across the country and take things as they come without feeling guilty?"

After a beat, one corner of Devon's mouth lifted into a half-smile. "You get what you want a lot, don't you?"

"Yes," Kylie answered without a trace of apology.

"Guess arguing with you would be kind of pointless, then," Devon said, pressing his forehead against hers for a brief second before lowering his lips for an equally quick kiss.

"Mmm hmm." Her belly squeezed with warmth and goodness and about forty other things as she kissed him back. But they had enough to worry about with Fagan just waiting for his chance to pounce. Complicating things between them? Yeah, that just seemed stupid.

"Now why don't you finish getting your stuff packed up while I grab a couple of waters from the vending machine?" Kylie asked. "Then we can get back on the road and take a dent out of some of this trip."

"We'll hit the vending machine together on the way out," Devon challenged, but Kylie had already grabbed a couple of dollar bills from her purse.

"It's literally ten feet from our front door. Plus, faster is better, remember?"

"Fast might be good, but safe is better." Devon took a nasty-looking knife out of the nightstand drawer, tucking it into the side pocket of his duffel as easily as if the thing were a butter knife going into a drawer. "I don't want you out of my sight."

A soft laugh pushed past Kylie's lips. "Everything worked out just fine when we did divide and conquer at the convenience store earlier."

"That was a mistake." His knuckles turned white over the nylon strap in his grasp, his spine unfolding into a rigid line. "I should never have let it happen. I won't fuck up like that again."

Kylie had closed the space between them before she even registered her brain's command to move. "Hey. We were barely separated in that mini-mart, and technically, you could see me the whole time. Plus, the whole thing went without a hitch. You're being a little hard on yourself, don't you think?"

"I think I'm not hard on myself nearly enough."

"What happened to you on your last tour in Afghanistan, Devon?"

Her cheeks burned at the brash question that had flown from her mouth, but there was no sense trying to take it back. What's more, she didn't want to. He hadn't exactly been a chatty guy when she'd met him five years ago, sure, but the titanium intensity and all of these scalpel-sharp edges were definitely new acquisitions.

Whatever had gone down out there in the desert had changed him. Not a little.

Devon opened his mouth, and for a second, Kylie thought he'd actually answer. But then the flash of emotion disappeared from his amber stare, and all at once, he was as unreadable as ancient Greek.

"Nothing. Look"—he shifted back to run a hand over his crew cut—"Fagan's dangerous as hell, and the thought of him trying to hurt you makes me want to kick the shit out of something. So until his ass is in a maximum security lockup where it belongs, you're going to have to get used to being stuck with me, okay?"

"Okay."

"What?" Devon's brows climbed in undisguised shock, but Kylie was done fighting the reality of her situation.

Xavier Fagan wanted her dead, and despite Devon's fierce demeanor and arm's length attitude, she trusted him one hundred percent to keep that from happening.

"If going together is the safest plan, then that's what we'll do," she said. Taking a step back, she gave him enough space to finish getting his things into the duffel bag, not even flinching as he slid his gun into the holster beneath his arm. Devon opened the curtains, scanning the mostly-empty parking lot with care before moving to open the door.

"Come on," he said, his voice as soft as the rest of him was tough. "Let's get you closer to that spaghetti dinner."

"Now that sounds like a plan." Kylie pressed her smile between her lips, squaring her shoulders beneath her white cotton tank top. Popping her aviator sunglasses over her face, she followed Devon's lead to the vending machine, relieved to see that her sly glances around the parking lot revealed nothing suspicious. She took the two bottles of water he passed in her direction, turning to make her way to the car so they could get the hell out of Dodge...

And ran smack into the motel manager.

"Oh!" Kylie exclaimed, her pulse going from zero to six thousand as she dropped one of the water bottles to the dingy pavement in surprise. The guy was stealthy as hell for someone who stank so badly, and she let out an involuntary cough at the lungful of smoke he'd just exhaled into her air space.

"Sorry about that. I was just getting a drink on my smoke break. Didn't mean to sneak up on you."

He offered up a crooked, yellow-tinged smile, and God, could she be any jumpier?

"Oh, no. It was my fault." She retrieved the bottle at her feet, tucking it into her purse along with the one she'd managed to hold on to.

"Aw, you're not in a hurry to leave us, are you?" the manager asked, his glance taking an obvious slide over the duffel on Devon's shoulder along with the keys in his hand. "You just got here a coupl'a hours ago. It's not even dinnertime yet."

"We're passing through," Devon said, clipping his tone close enough to the quick that the manager held up both hands in concession.

"Okay, no need to get uppity. Just thought maybe you and Kylie might want to stay and relax a little while longer."

Every last hair on the back of Kylie's neck stood at attention all at once. "How do you know my name?"

"Oh." The manager's smile slipped. "Uh, your boyfriend here must have said it when you two were checking in."

In less than a blink, Devon swung the man around, pinning him to the vending machine with a graceless *thunk*.

"No. I didn't. Try again."

The manager sputtered, his bloodshot eyes bulging. "Guess she just looks like a Kylie. Must be that pretty face."

"Don't insult me, or I'll get pissed off." Devon pressed a thick forearm over the man's windpipe, and oh God, oh God, oh God, Kylie wanted to get out of here, like yesterday.

"Okay. Okay!" the manager choked, his wild-eyed stare flattening on her over the hard angle of Devon's shoulder. "Fagan's coming for her, and he wants blood. There's nothing you can do. His network is huge, and he's got everyone within five hundred miles looking—"

"When?" Devon leaned harder, his body language an unspoken embodiment of *don't fuck with me*.

The manager's lips peeled back in a thin grimace. "Now."

Devon dropped the man into a heap on the sidewalk. "Kylie, get in the car. Go."

He didn't have to tell her twice. She ran to the Challenger, flinging the passenger door open hard enough to make the hinges protest. Throwing herself inside, she slammed the door in her wake, her breath coming in such rapid bursts that she was certain she'd either pass out or throw up.

Devon shoved his duffel in the back seat and punched the key into the ignition, sweeping the parking lot with a cold, glittering stare. "Get down as far as you can," he said, the words barely reaching Kylie's ears past the roar of the engine as he pulled out of the parking lot.

"Do you see anything?" she asked, unable to just sit there, quiet and helpless.

"Not yet, but that doesn't mean nothing's there." He maneuvered the car through a turn, although toward what, Kylie had no clue.

Oh, screw this. "Let me help," she said, sitting up in her seat to take in their sun-drenched surroundings. "I can keep watch out the back window while you get us out of here."

"No. You need to stay safe." Devon split his attention between the road and the rearview, but managing both views had to be the mother of all balancing acts.

Kylie refused to budge. "I get that this road is pretty empty, but we're not going to be very safe if you wreck the car, Devon. Believe me, if bullets start flying, I'll be the first person to hit the damned deck. But for now, I'm helping."

Whether it was for her attitude or her argument, she didn't know, but Devon gave in with a swear. "Fine. We're going to backtrack for a few miles, then try to pick up an alternate route to South Dakota. If you see anyone—*anyone*—behind us, you need to say so. Got it?"

"Got it." Kylie did a one-eighty against the passenger seat, trying to recalibrate her pulse to something that vaguely resembled normal as she stared through the back windshield. Small houses dotted either side of the dusty, two-lane back highway, the road bisected here and there by a handful of narrow cross streets and hidden driveways.

A minute passed, then two. Devon fired up the GPS device he'd hauled from the trunk earlier this morning, bringing up their location and mapping out an eastward route as he drove.

"Okay. According to this, we can take this road in a straight shot until we get to—"

Oh. God. "Devon." Fear slipped down Kylie's spine with cold, clammy fingers. "A red pickup truck just pulled out from that cross street, and it's catching up to us, fast."

She turned toward him at the same time his gaze arrowed in on the rearview mirror, and he ditched the GPS in favor of pulling his gun from its holster.

"Hold on, and be ready to take the wheel if I tell you to."

Devon slammed his boot over the accelerator, the car rocketing down the empty back road fast enough to make Kylie's stomach drop all the way to her hips. With her heart lodged somewhere in the vicinity of her voice box, she reached behind her, pulling her seat belt over her chest while still keeping her eyes trained on the pickup truck behind them.

How the hell had it gotten *closer?*

"Devon." She'd barely gotten the word past her lips when a figure leaned out of the truck's passenger window, aiming a trio of rapid-fire shots in the direction of the Challenger.

"Holy shit!" Kylie cried, ducking behind her seat. Although the shots seemed to have missed the car completely, the urge to panic still flared to life in her veins.

But then Devon pinned her with a sure, cool stare, jerking his chin at the steering wheel. "I need you to take the wheel, Kylie. Just stay as low as you can and keep us on the road. You with me?"

Her nod was a default even though she was fifty-fifty at backing it up. "Just steer and watch the road? What are you going to do?"

Devon's answer was the click of his gun's safety and the whoosh of the driver's side window disappearing into the doorframe. Kylie bit down on her lip, forcing herself to stare out the windshield in front of them. The road was pretty straight as far as she could see, and she leaned in to grip the leather-wrapped steering wheel from the passenger seat.

"Got it," she called over the whipping wind. Devon shifted his body so his left boot replaced his right on the accelerator, twisting around to lean the right side of his body out the open window while his left foot still mashed down on the gas.

Spaghetti, meatballs, wine, and a double freaking helping of tiramisu. Kylie screamed the words in her head, commanding both hands to stay locked on the Challenger's wheel. Devon squeezed off two shots with a loud *pop-pop*, and she sent up a prayer that one of them would hit something vital in the pickup truck.

Nope.

"Keep steering," Devon yelled, readjusting in a blur. Three more shots blasted from his gun, the unmistakable screech of rubber against pavement telling Kylie he must've bull's-eyed one of the pickup's tires. A jumble of loud, indecipherable sounds flew in through the window, but only after Devon had slid back into the driver's seat a minute later did she allow herself to turn and look.

"Holy mother of..." The pickup truck had banked hard and spun off the pavement. Although the hulking vehicle was upright, it stood at an unnatural angle on the deeply pitched shoulder of the road, clearly out of commission.

"Are you okay?" Devon asked, his knuckles flashing white against the steering wheel as he darted a quick glance at her face. "Dammit, Kylie. You're bleeding."

"What? No I'm not, I'm—ow." The sting of her bottom lip didn't register until he reached out to skim it with a gentle touch, but jeez, that hurt.

"You must've bit your lip."

Kylie resisted the weird compulsion to laugh. "If that's the worst thing that happens to me, I'll take it and run. Do you think they'll be able to follow us?"

"Not in that truck." Devon threw a hard look at the rearview. "But this changes things. We'll need to keep moving until Kellan can get some help our way."

"Okay," she said, sitting on her hands to keep them from shaking. *You've got this. Devon's got this.* "So what's our next step?"

Devon reached out to swipe a fast-food napkin from the glove box, pressing it into her hand while eagle-eyeing the road both in front of them and behind. "Thankfully, we have enough gas that we won't need to stop for another two hundred miles, maybe more. We're going to have to drive in shifts, but we should be able to make decent time to South Dakota."

"You want me to help?" Kylie's jaw fell open.

"I want to keep you safe," Devon corrected. "But the best way to do that is to work as a team, so yeah." He grabbed her fingers, and Kylie felt the squeeze all the way from her breastbone to her boots.

"I want you to help."

Chapter Eight

Devon's eyes burned like they'd been dipped in battery acid and set out in the sun to dry, but he blinked twice, ignoring the sensation. Levering his foot a little harder over the gas pedal, he stared through the windshield, watching the irony of a gorgeous sunrise over the horizon.

Fagan was going down. The uglier, the better.

Devon was going to make sure of it.

"Looks like we should make it to Iowa City in about fifteen minutes," Kylie said, her slender brows tucking into a V as she looked at the GPS. "By then maybe we'll have heard something from Kellan."

"He was pretty set on getting out here today. I'm sure he's working something out with that detective contact of his to get you into protective custody ASAP."

Translation: Kellan had probably been in the woman's face 24/7 ever since Devon had dropped the news that they'd been shot at leaving Montana yesterday afternoon. It had taken all of Devon's negotiation skills to convince the guy not to just jump on a plane all yippy-ki-yay and start blasting his way through the Midwest. While the idea of ending Fagan had a metric ton of merit, stepping strategically was important now more than ever.

Devon had sworn to keep Kylie safe, and come hellfire or brimstone, he was going to be a man of his word.

The shrill ring of his cell phone cut through the quiet in the

Challenger, and speak of the sinner. "Walker. Tell me you have a plan."

"I do," Kellan said, pausing only long enough for Devon to put him on speaker so Kylie could be part of the convo before continuing. "How far are you from Chicago?"

"Um." Kylie's fingers flew over the backlit screen of the GPS. "About two hundred miles, give or take."

Kellan let out a relieved exhale. "The NCPD arranged for me to fly under an alias, so Moreno and I are getting on a plane in three hours. She knows a DEA agent at the field office in Chicago, and she says the guy and his unit are good police. They can bring Kylie into protective custody and keep her safe while they hunt Fagan down."

Whoa. Talk about bringing in the big guns. Literally *and* figuratively. "Copy that." Devon paused, considering taking Kellan off speaker for the next part, but screw it. Kylie was tough enough to handle the truth, and anyway, she deserved full disclosure. "How do you want to work this? Because I'll be honest. Your detective might trust this DEA guy, but the only person I trust in this scenario is you."

"You think I'll still be in danger once we get to a DEA field office in a major city?" Kylie asked, and Kellan made a sound to match her disbelief.

"I don't know, Dev. I get that Fagan had a lot of locals in his pocket, but Chicago's a far cry from Podunk. You really think the guy's got hooks like that?"

Devon's gaze landed on Kylie, and something fierce and dark turned over in his belly. "I really think we can't take the chance."

A few heartbeats passed before Kellan said, "Okay. Get to Chicago and lay low. I'll reach out once Moreno and I land and we'll strike a rendezvous point with the DEA. They're not going to like the plan, but I'm not in it for a popularity contest. Just stay under the radar 'til I get there."

"Copy that."

Kellan's response came after a pause that said he'd been measuring his words. "Hey, Ky, can you pick up for a second?"

Kylie's blue eyes narrowed, but she reached for the cell phone

Devon had propped up over the dash. Cradling it to her ear, she mostly listened, adding a couple of quiet "mmm hmm"s to the mix before disconnecting the call.

"Everything okay?" Devon asked, although man, considering the threat level involved in their circumstances, the question was pretty brainless.

"Yeah." Kylie wrapped her arms around her midsection, looking at the pink and orange-tinged landscape outside the passenger window. "He's just worried. Wanted to make sure I'm hanging in there."

Devon's gut squeezed as if someone had jammed it into a vise. Of course Kellan would go out of his way to make sure Kylie was straight. She was in danger. Her life was on the line.

And the only person keeping watch over her was Devon, who had nearly gotten a bullet buried in his buddy's skull.

If you move, I will kill your friend. You'll watch him die screaming, and then I'll kill you just as slowly.

"Right. Of course," Devon managed, his shoulders going stiff against the black leather of the driver's seat. Dammit, he needed to put a stranglehold on that memory, once and for all. "Well, Chicago is only five hours from here. If you want to close your eyes, I'm good to drive."

"Devon, what happened on your last tour in Afghanistan?"

The answer burned in his chest, begging for release just as it had when she'd asked the same question yesterday. For four years, he'd kept the whole thing buried, covering his unworthiness and guilt by holding everyone at a distance. Devon had grown tough not because he liked it—hell, half the time he looked in the mirror, he didn't even recognize his reflection. He'd grown hard-edged and cold out of necessity. To get through the freelance jobs. To be there when the guys at MacKenzie Security needed him. To cope.

But he couldn't tell Kylie any of these things. He needed her to trust him for a little while longer, just until he made sure she was safe.

And if Devon told her the truth, her trust in him would shatter. No matter how badly he wanted to tell her every last bit of the horrible truth he'd kept buried.

Hell, he really wanted to tell her. But her trust would keep her safe, and right now, he needed that more.

"Afghanistan was a long time ago. It's in the past," he said, keeping his gaze fixed firmly on the road, his mind set on keeping her protected.

But when she finally turned toward the window and closed her eyes in defeated silence, Devon couldn't shake the feeling that if he'd told Kylie everything, she'd have understood.

* * * *

They made record time to Chicago, thanks in no small part to Devon's determination to get there and get hidden. Kylie had slept for pretty much the duration of the ride to the motel on the outskirts of the city, and he'd spent the time trying—and failing—to knock back his thoughts of the past.

He knew he needed to focus on the present now more than ever. But with how Kylie was looking at him, so wide open and strong and so damn beautiful as she chained the motel room door and immediately closed the curtains like he'd taught her, Devon could no longer deny the truth hammered home by the five-hour drive.

What had happened in Afghanistan *had* happened. He could never atone for it, but if he didn't give himself some breathing room, making good on Kylie's trust in the here and now would never truly happen.

And he needed it. He needed *her.*

He needed to tell her.

"Devon?" Kylie's voice threaded past the slam of his heartbeat against his ears. "What's the matter?"

"I…there was an ambush. In Afghanistan."

Devon blinked, the words sounding strange out loud after having been buried for so long. But now that he'd flipped the lid on the memory, the whole thing rushed upward, pushing and burning and desperate to be told.

Kylie crossed the carpet, standing in front of him in an instant even though she said nothing, just looked at him with trust in her eyes, listening.

And hell if that didn't make the words flow out faster.

"We were doing a routine sweep in a village we'd been to dozens of times. The place was remote, but so was pretty much everything else we saw in the desert. There were no signs of a threat—we practically knew the village by heart. Everything was good to go. Business as usual."

Air like an oven, almost too hot to breathe…sunlight slashing past the glassless windows in the mud-brick walls, throwing patterns on the dirt floors…

Everything had seemed so fucking normal. Right up until it wasn't.

Devon cleared his throat. "A lot of times, insurgents hide in plain sight, blending in with the friendlies so they can get close to US soldiers. They don't discriminate. Women, the elderly, kids. The insurgents would strong-arm anyone if it meant getting close enough to hurt us, which is why we swept the places pretty regularly. Part of our job was to keep the friendlies safe."

Inhale. Exhale. Get the story out. "Kellan and I paired off to check one of the dwellings in the village. The locals used the place as a school of sorts."

"Were…were there kids inside?" Kylie whispered, but he read the fear in her eyes and shook his head. At least he could reassure her of one good thing.

"No," he said, and Kylie's relief-tinged breath out was warm as it coasted over his cheek. "The school was nearly empty. That wasn't totally unusual because it was a little late in the day. One of the local men who taught the kids was there, though. He greeted us, invited us in, then left. I checked the back room, and everything looked solid."

Guilt and regret flooded Devon's veins, making his hands shake at his sides. But rather than shy away from the story that she had to know had no happy ending, Kylie laced her fingers through his, holding strong.

"Everything wasn't okay, though, was it?"

"No. There was a hostile who'd been hiding in the back. I swear I never saw any sign of him. He grabbed me from behind and put a gun to my head. Then he said something I'll never forget."

The cold pressure of steel against his sweat-slicked temple…the steady, evil voice sliding from Devon's ear to the center of his chest, so clear and so deadly, he could still hear every syllable, every inflection…

If you move, I will kill your friend. You'll watch him die screaming, and then I'll kill you just as slowly. Your men will come running, and they too will die. All of you will die today.

Kylie sucked in a breath, and only then did Devon realize he'd relayed the man's threat out loud.

"So what did you do?" she asked, her tone wobbly despite what looked like a Grade-A effort to stay steady.

"I didn't do anything," Devon said past the pounding of his heart against his rib cage. "Kellan shot the guy dead without so much as blinking. He saved both our lives—*all* our lives—and all I did was stand there."

Kylie's lips parted. "Devon, you were being held at gunpoint. Of course you just stood there. If you'd fought back, that psycho would've killed you." Abruptly, understanding lit like a switch in her eyes. "You blame yourself for that ambush, don't you? You think it was your fault you and Kellan were in harm's way."

He took a step back on the carpet, his frustration going from a simmer to a boil. "Of course it was my fault. I did the sweep! There had to have been a sign, something I missed somewhere." Devon had been over that day so many times, the details were permanently etched in his memory.

"There wasn't," Kylie said, pinning him with a stare that cut off the protest she must've seen brewing in his expression. "You're meticulous to a fault. If that insurgent had left even the slightest hint he was there waiting, you'd have seen it."

Funny, Kellan had said the same thing, over and over. Still… "I risked every one of my teammate's lives that day, including your brother's. I don't deserve his trust, or yours."

"And yet you have it from both of us."

Her words startled Devon so thoroughly that all he could do was gape like a Neanderthal while she continued. "I know I'll never forget how terrified I was when Fagan put that gun to my head, and I can only imagine how much worse it was for you, with that threat extending to other people you cared about. But the man to blame died in that village. *He's* the bad guy. Not you."

Kylie let go of his hands, her palms coasting up to frame his face, and Christ, when she looked at him like that, he wanted so badly to believe her. "I should've seen him. I—"

"There was nothing to see."

"How can you be so sure?" he asked, the words little more than a hoarse whisper in the quiet motel room.

"Because you keep me steady when all I want to do is fall apart. You're calm and smart and sure, and I know in my heart you'd do anything to keep me safe." Her arms slipped around him, and Christ, no one had ever felt so good there, so right. "I don't just trust you, Devon. I need you. No matter what happened in the past, or what happens after today, I only need you."

Chapter Nine

Kylie lifted her mouth to Devon's without hesitation. She might not know how to convince him he was worthy, or if she could come up with any words that could accurately describe how she felt in this moment. But the guilt pouring out of him nearly gutted her, and she had to do something—anything—to show him what she knew by heart.

Devon would keep her safe. He would keep her steady.

Kylie trusted him with her life.

His arms wrapped around her in a flash. Returning the chaste press of her lips with a desperate bid for more, he quickly took the kiss from a whisper to a scream. Devon parted her mouth, searching and taking with his tongue, his lips pushed so hard over hers that she ached. But the more urgent he got, the more Kylie gave back, her tongue sliding over his, diving deep before retreating to let him have control.

She reached into the tight sliver of space between them, her fingers curling over the black cotton hem of Devon's T-shirt. Heat moved in a straight shot between her thighs, but he caught her hands, stopping her movements.

"Kylie. I'm not—"

"You are." She cut him off before he could say the words *good enough*. His eyes blazed like fire-lit whiskey, full of his own burning need, and in that split second, Kylie's realization settled in, hard and fast.

All the words in the universe wouldn't work. She needed to *show* Devon she trusted him.

With all of her.

Kylie took a step back. With quick moves, she toed out of her boots, reaching down to remove her clothes until she stood in front of the bed in nothing but her bra and panties.

"What are you doing?" Devon asked, the words gravel over silk.

"I'm showing you what I see." She climbed onto the bed, tugging back the comforter to expose the plain, white sheets. Her pulse beat a needful rhythm against her breastbone, and she reclined against the pillows to meet his questioning stare.

"I don't understand."

"Do you want me, Devon?"

"Yes." His jaw turned to granite in the lamplight spilling down from behind him. "Hell, yes."

Kylie smiled, her own desire spilling all the way through her as she said, "Then take me. Touch me, kiss me, fuck me any way you want. I trust you."

A groan slipped past Devon's lips, but he didn't hesitate. Pulling his T-shirt over his head, he took off his clothes—shirt, boots, jeans—and dear, sweet Lord, his body was perfect. For a minute, he stood there in front of her in nothing but a pair of black boxer briefs, as if he sensed Kylie's need to simply take him in.

And so she did. Smooth, tanned skin covered the tight angles of his shoulders and the solid, muscular plane of his chest. His abs showcased enough definition to be sexy, but not so much that he looked fake. No gym had cultivated these muscles, uh-uh. Devon's body was a testament to hard work, to running miles on perimeter checks, not treadmills. Kylie's gaze trailed lower, over the corded V sculpting either side of his hips and the outline of his fully erect cock beneath the fabric in between. Her nipples tightened and pressed against the lace of her bra, the friction sending a tremor directly to her clit.

"You want me to touch you," he said. The words held no question, but Kylie answered anyway.

"Yes." She nodded, her hair swishing around her cheeks, as

wild and unfettered as she felt. Devon moved to the side of the bed, close enough to run a hand from her wrist to her shoulder to the slope of her neck, and she was helpless to do anything other than arch into his touch.

Devon's fingers found her cheekbone, his palm fitting reverently over her jaw as he stroked her bottom lip with his thumb. "You're still swollen here, from where you bit yourself." Back and forth, his thumb moved, the motion gentle on her tender skin. "Does it hurt?"

"A little," she admitted, although she parted her lips wider to accommodate his hypnotic movement. Pain, pleasure, pain, pleasure...the sensations melted together, both of them heightening her arousal, doubling the need under her skin. "But I like it when you touch me."

He didn't stop. Sitting next to her on the bed, he slid the pad of his thumb to the indent at the center of her lips, pressing slowly into the wet heat of her mouth.

Kylie moaned, opening to let her tongue caress the warm, callused skin of his thumb. But rather than letting her engage, Devon retreated to the spot where her lip met her chin.

"I want to really touch you. Not where you have to do anything back." His thumb edged back to where it had been, her nerve endings dancing like little live wires in anticipation, her sex growing wet at the suggestion of his simple touch on her mouth and nothing more. "But where all you do is feel. Will you let me do that, Kylie? Just close your eyes and let me in?"

"Yes."

She opened her lips as her eyes fluttered closed. Devon stroked and swept, his fingers hooking beneath her chin while his thumb ignited tiny sparks with every touch. His movements grew more provocative, the tip of his thumb sliding into her mouth, teasing her tongue with a tiny flick before drawing back out. Kylie's breath came faster, pushing out of her lungs, and oh, oh God, she felt his ministrations everywhere. The salt of his skin was heady on her tongue, his thumb teasing her mouth with just enough pressure to drive her crazy, and she bowed up from the pillows, in search of more.

"Devon," Kylie panted, her eyes springing open, and he raked her body with a slow, white-hot stare.

"You want me to kiss you next," he said, repeating back her words from when she'd first lay down in front of him.

Suddenly, "yes" seemed like the most lacking word on the planet, but she said it anyway. Devon's fingers moved from her mouth, joined by his other hand as he skimmed his touch to her hips.

"Jesus, Kylie. Look how pretty you are." He pressed closer to her on the bedsheets, and she tucked her chin to follow his warm-whiskey gaze between her legs. Her white cotton panties rode the bare, sensitive flesh beneath, the material transparent from the slick heat of her pussy, but Kylie didn't feel vulnerable or self-conscious at the obvious proof of her arousal.

"You like to watch," Devon said, dragging a finger over the fabric-covered seam of her sex. "You want to watch me kiss you?"

Her clit throbbed, her knees falling wide. "Yes."

"Then keep your eyes wide open, sweetheart. Because I'm not kissing your mouth, and I'm not getting up until you come."

In the span of a few pounding heartbeats, Devon had pulled off her panties and settled his body between her thighs. Kylie's legs shook with need as he hooked one arm beneath the curve of her ass, his fingers splaying wide over her belly as he lowered his mouth to her sex.

She nearly came out of her skin from the warm, wet contact. "Oh...*God.*" Kylie tilted her hips, her clit aching for the press of his tongue, but Devon held steady.

"Keep watching," he said. His free hand dusted over her inner thigh, fingers playing momentarily in the crease dividing her leg and her body before sliding in to part the folds of her sex. Spreading her wide, Devon teased her in long strokes, learning her with his lips and tongue. Heat built deep at the center of her hips, although whether it was from the highly intimate way he was kissing her or the fact that she was watching his every move as he did it, Kylie didn't know. Didn't care. Didn't feel anything that wasn't Devon's mouth, working her pussy with hot, hard flicks of his tongue.

She tried to form words to tell him how good he felt, but they came out no more than pleasured moans. Her hands reached down, one digging into the arm Devon had locked over her belly, the other cradling his head as he pumped his tongue into her sex. His expression was the perfect combination of reverence and intensity, making Kylie's heart beat faster and the heat in her body explode. He shifted, sucking her clit past his lips in a sweet, punishing draw, and she came with a cry. Turning her nails into the hard muscles of Devon's arm, she levered off the bed, pulsing and praying and unraveling until she'd run out of breath.

"Did you mean what you said?" Devon asked a minute later, his voice vibrating against her still-sensitive sex. He pulled back to look at her. His eyes flared, both bright and wicked, but Kylie nodded without a second thought.

"I did." She slid over the bedsheets, propping herself on her knees in front of him.

He raised up to meet her, lowering his boxer briefs to free his rock-hard cock from the cotton. "You want me to fuck you any way I want."

Desire rekindled between her legs at the thought. "I trust you, Devon." She circled his length with her fingers, pumping up and down. "I'm yours. All you have to do is take me."

Pausing only long enough to grab a condom and put it on, Devon gripped Kylie's hips. His hard angles and tanned skin stood out against her creamy curves, but she loved the way his hands looked on her.

And then suddenly, she couldn't see them, because he'd swung her around on her bed so her back was pressed up against his chest.

"I know watching turns you on," he said, his breath ragged as it warmed her neck, her shoulder. "But it turns me on, too."

Kylie let out a soft gasp. "Then watch," she said. Widening her knees, she bent forward, leaning until her palms spread open over the flat expanse of the headboard.

Devon's fingers tightened on her hips. He loosened one hand, using it to guide his cock to the slippery wetness at her entrance.

But he didn't press forward to fill her. "Gorgeous," he murmured, and the slight brush of contact made her inner muscles clench. Finally, he sank into her inch by inch, filling her body until his hips were flush against her ass.

"Kylie." His voice filled her ears as he drew back, thrusting forward to stretch her again. Sensations ricocheted through Kylie's body, then her brain, then her body again, each one turning her want into sheer, limitless need.

She spread her legs farther, a dark thrill shooting through her blood as he moaned, pumping harder. "Yes. Don't hold back, Devon."

"Christ, Kylie. You're so damned tight." He thrust again and again, hitting every sweet spot inside her. Their rhythm went from slow build to fast burn, making another climax flicker to life between her legs. She hinged all the way forward, taking him deeper, and when she reached between her legs to stroke her clit as he fucked her, their moans crashed together.

"That's it. Touch yourself. Feel everything." Devon slowed his motions, and for a second, she nearly protested. But then Kylie looked over her shoulder, watching him change the tempo of how he fucked her to meet the movements of her greedy fingers, and oh God, it was the hottest thing she'd ever seen or felt. Friction combined with pressure, both spiraling faster and stronger and hotter until she tumbled over the edge of her climax.

Devon tightened behind her, his cock buried to the hilt. "Ah. *Ah*, God."

Keeping him all the way inside, she bucked her hips against his, letting him feel the squeeze of her pussy as her orgasm ended and his began. His spine arched, his strong, hard body beginning to shake as he called her name again and again.

And in that second, Kylie knew that she didn't just trust Devon enough to give him her body.

She trusted him enough to fall for him.

* * * *

Kylie dried her hair as best she could with the motel bath towel, ruffling her fingers through the tawny brown waves one last time before calling it as good as it got. She was starting to get used to the change—liked it better than the pink, actually. But one thing she'd never get used to was being on the run.

Thank God the terrifying part was almost over.

"Hey." Devon appeared in the doorway to the bathroom that she'd left open while she'd showered, a protein bar in hand. "I know these are less than appealing, especially for someone who likes to cook, but you really should eat something."

"Thanks," she said, brushing a quick kiss over his mouth before taking the yellow and red package from his hand. "Have you heard anything from Kellan?" Her brother's flight was scheduled to land at any minute, and as soon as he was on the ground in Chicago, things would get crazy really fast.

An image of Devon flashed through her mind, his hands on her body and his face caught up in the intensity of his release, and okay, some things might already be a little crazy.

But God, he felt right.

"No," Devon said, bringing Kylie back to the reality of the here and now. "But as soon as he and Detective Moreno land and they reach out, this DEA guy and his unit can take you into protective custody."

Kylie's pulse picked up in her veins, and she followed Devon back to the main room, sitting on the edge of the bed. "So, um, what happens after that?"

He pulled on a fresh T-shirt, his hands staying busy as he spoke. "They'll keep you in a safe house until they can pick Fagan up. The guy's drug activity is legendary, and with the murder you witnessed, the chances he'll see the light of day again are pretty much nil."

"Fagan's never been caught before." She fiddled with the protein bar wrapper, hating the fear pinging through her chest. "Do you think he'll run?"

"Probably," Devon said, although his tone marked the word as a definite.

"So I might be in protective custody for a while."

He paused. "I'd say there's a pretty high likelihood of that, yes. But it's to keep you safe."

"You'll be there, then. Right?" she asked, and his chin snapped up, his eyes going wide.

"Probably not. MacKenzie Security is good—the best, actually. But the DEA never farms out their protective custody cases. It's too risky."

Kylie's pulse began to pound beneath her tank top. "But I'm the witness. What about what I want? You're a former Army Ranger, for God's sake, and you work for the best private security company around. Look"—she tossed her protein bar to the bed, crossing the room to the spot where Devon stood—"I don't want to take risks either. But if the DEA wants me safe, the best person...no, the *only* person to put me with is you."

Kylie measured the silence that followed in heartbeats and breaths, and finally Devon pulled her close.

"Okay. Kellan and I will talk to Detective Moreno and her contact. See what we can work out. Your brother is going to kick my ass for this." He dropped his lips to her forehead, his kiss soft. "But I want you safe, Kylie. I want you."

Her response was cut off by the ring of Devon's cell phone, and he unwound his arms to pull the thing from the pocket of his jeans. "Randolph."

Kylie's stomach pitched, and ugh, she should've eaten that stupid protein bar. She listened carefully, although Devon's end of the conversation was mostly a series of "affirmative"s and "negative"s. He capped the conversation with the address and room number they were currently standing in, though, so everything must've been going according to plan.

"Well?" she asked the nanosecond Devon had lowered the phone.

"We're good to go. Kellan and Moreno are on their way from the airport. ETA fifteen minutes." He slid his phone back into his pocket, breaking into a small smile. "Guess you should start thinking about that spaghetti dinner, huh?"

She smiled back, feeling the warmth to her toes. "Only if it's for two."

They spent a few minutes gathering the handful of things they'd brought with them, tidying the room to erase all signs that they'd been there. Devon slipped into the bathroom, and Kylie tightened the laces on her boots in the very definition of ready to go.

She was headed for safety. *Real* safety. With Devon at her side.

A tap sounded off on the door, sending her pulse through the stratosphere. But the sound was followed by a deep, quiet voice saying, "DEA," and Kylie's breath whooshed out in relief.

"Oh thank God," she murmured, unchaining the door to pull it open. "We thought you'd—"

The rest of her sentence was swallowed by a rough hand over her mouth. Ripping pain exploded through her head, and the last thing Kylie saw before she slipped into blackness was Xavier Fagan's cold, dead stare.

Chapter Ten

Devon took his backup weapon out from behind the toilet, giving the nine mil a quick clean-and-check before sticking it in his waistband at the small of his back. Normally, he didn't go that route, preferring not to shoot his own ass off by accident, but even with the SIG in his side holster and the butterfly knife in his boot, he wasn't about to be too careful.

Kylie trusted him to keep her safe. And for the first time in four years, he trusted himself one hundred percent, too. Yeah, her being in protective custody was going to suck, but he knew Kellan. His buddy wouldn't stop dogging the DEA until Fagan was behind bars and razor wire, and if the MacKenzies were able to pull a few strings, with any luck, Devon could keep eyes on Kylie until that happened.

Guys like him weren't supposed to have luck, but damn, today sure felt like his day.

He opened the door, stepping into the motel room. "Okay, we've only got a few minutes, so—"

His words crashed like a ten-car pileup at the sight of Xavier Fagan with a gun to Kylie's head and his greasy hand clapped over her mouth.

"Ah-ah-ah," Fagan said, pressing his snub-nosed Glock harder against Kylie's temple as Devon's muscle memory jerked his hand in search of his gun. "I'll be needing that weapon of yours on the bed. Whatever's in your boot, too."

Devon cursed, his stomach going low and tight as he scanned Kylie for injuries. Blood trickled down from her hairline, but only enough to suggest a small wound. She was conscious, her blue eyes glassy and wide, and goddamn it, Devon was going to dismember Fagan for putting his hands on her.

"Okay," Devon said, his tactical options rolling through his skull at warp speed. Time. He needed to stall until Kellan arrived with the cavalry. "Just give me a minute."

"You have ten seconds, or I'm going to redecorate this room with what's inside your girl's pretty little head."

Kylie's whimper kicked Devon into gear. He slipped out of his holster, tossing the SIG onto the bedsheets, heel-toeing his shit-kickers to the carpet in front of him.

"Happy?" he asked, holding his hands at his side in concession.

Fagan's laugh curled around the air like a filthy dishrag. "Let's see. I damn near had my nose broken, courtesy of this dirty whore"—his grip over Kylie's body dug tighter at the mention of the blue-black bruise swelling beneath one eye—"I've wasted manpower and money chasing your asses all over the fucking map, and I had to cash in the mother of all favors in order to finally nail your location. Fucking DEA agents. They might be good, but they're not goddamn cheap."

Realization cemented Devon's breath to his lungs. "You bought off one of the agents on the field team?"

"Circle gets the square," Fagan said, his voice overloaded with sarcasm. "You think just because we're in a big city, DEA agents can't be bought? Shit. I've got news for you, Randolph. Everyone can be bought. Kinda like the clerk at the county office three towns over from Surrender. Told me all about that sister of yours. How many kids does she have with that husband of hers now? Three? No, wait—four. How could I forget that sweet doll Greta?"

It took every last ounce of his self-restraint not to just say fuck it and try to murder Fagan with his bare hands. "You've made your point."

"Have I? Because I want to be sure you know exactly how this is going to shake out. I've got five, maybe six minutes before the DEA swarms this place. Which means I only have two to kill the both of you. Lover's quarrel." Fagan paused, clicking his tongue to the roof of his mouth. "So sad. But if either one of you fights me, or even so much as looks at me sideways, I'm going to make sure both your sister and that pain in the ass Kellan have very unfortunate accidents."

Kylie's eyes rounded in terror, as if she were finally shaking off a fog. Her body tensed, her steps jerky as Fagan kicked at her feet to steer her farther into the center of the room.

If you move...

...I'll kill you just as slowly...

All of you will die today.

No. No.

Kylie trusted him. He trusted himself. All Devon needed was an opening.

Which, of course, he didn't have.

"Don't worry, sweetheart," Fagan said, loosening his grip on Kylie just enough to stick her with a glittering black stare. "I'll even do you first so we can get this over with quick. Remember what I said about making a fuss. You scream, and I'll gut your brother like a pig."

He took his hand off Kylie's mouth, and her eyes landed on Devon's.

"I trust you," she whispered.

The gun was out of his waistband on pure, primal instinct. He registered the press of cold steel, the squeeze of his muscles forming one fluid move, the stop-motion image of the crease between Fagan's eyebrows.

Devon shot him between the eyes in the span of a heartbeat.

"Oh my God!" Kylie let out a sound somewhere between a scream and a sob. "Oh my God, oh my God. Devon!" She launched herself at him, her voice breaking with emotion and relief.

He put a quick visual on Fagan even though he knew he'd landed a kill shot, and yeah, the guy wasn't ever getting up. "Jesus, Kylie. Baby, let me look at you." Devon loosened his grip on his nine mil, his hands coasting over her in fear and relief.

"I'm okay," she said, although she let him turn her so her line of sight didn't include Fagan's body. "I'm—"

The door exploded inward on a burst of noise. "DEA! Don't move!"

Devon shielded Kylie, his gun back in hand within seconds. "My name is Devon Randolph, and this is your witness, Kylie Walker. Your man down is Xavier Fagan. The scene is secure."

Fortunately, nobody got chippy with him, because the next two people spilling through the door were a female detective and Kellan, both wearing Kevlar and both looking furious.

"Kylie!" Kellan elbowed past the agent who had stopped to secure Fagan's body, throwing his arms around his sister. "Shit, Ky, you're bleeding. Moreno, you need to roll an ambo out here, like now."

"I'm fine, Kellan. I mean, Fagan rang my bell a little, but all things considered, I think he got the worse end of the deal," she said.

Kellan chuffed out a laugh. "You must be okay if you're cracking wise."

The female detective, Moreno according to the nameplate on her Kevlar, grabbed a towel from the bathroom, passing it to Kellan so he could administer first aid. "What the hell happened here? How did Fagan find you?"

Kylie opened her mouth, but Devon cut her off before she could answer. "I'm not sure." He cut a glance at the three DEA agents, all within earshot, and no way was he going to let whichever one of them was dirty get away with putting Kylie's life at risk. "I must've been sloppy somewhere along the way."

"Bullshit," Kellan said at the same time Kylie flinched, but Devon continued despite the punch of emotion in his gut.

"Fagan muscled his way in, tried to grab Kylie. I took a lucky shot. That's about all there is to it."

Moreno frowned. "Pretty careless for someone who should know better. Not only did you risk Kylie's life, but now everyone working with Fagan will go deep underground. We'll probably never catch most of them."

"Hey," Kellan protested, but Devon put his hand on the guy's shoulder. This was hard enough as it was.

"You got Fagan. Now can we get out of here to give our

statements? Because you might not like them, but I think you're
going to want to hear them."

* * * *

Devon pushed back from the table in the interrogation room,
his chair scraping across the linoleum as he propped his forearms
over his thighs.

"So you're telling me Xavier Fagan paid off an agent in my unit
in order to obtain the location of a witness so he could murder her
in cold blood before we could take her into custody." Special Agent
Brett Collins, a.k.a. Detective Moreno's contact and head of the
DEA's field office in Chicago, looked at Devon with an unreadable
stare. "That's a pretty hefty accusation."

"I'm aware," Devon said, especially since he'd made the
accusation a half a dozen times since arriving at the field office four
hours ago. "But since my statement is the truth, I'm not going to be
changing it any time soon. No matter how many different ways you
ask me what went down."

"Mmm." Collins scrubbed a hand over his salt and pepper
goatee. "Well, Ms. Walker's story corroborates yours, and there was
a clear and present threat to her well-being. For now, I'm inclined
to let you walk. Provided that you agree not to disclose the details
of what Fagan told you to anyone."

Devon didn't envy the guy for the investigation he'd have to
launch into his own field officers' conduct, that was for damn sure.
"Of course. You don't think Kylie's still at risk, do you?"

"On the record, I'll tell you that I can't disclose any
information pertaining to the case. But off?" Collins paused, one
shoulder of his white dress shirt lifting in a half-shrug. "Fagan was
the head of the snake. Whoever his informant is will probably hide.
Not that it'll help when I get my hands on him."

Devon followed the man out of the interrogation room, his
pulse doing the hey-now in his veins as he spotted Kellan in the
main hallway.

"Hey. Jesus, I thought they were going to keep you in there all
month. Is everything okay?"

The entire chain of events kind of turned *okay* on its ear, but given the fact that he was too hungry, tired, and fried to make like a thesaurus, okay would have to do. "Yeah. How's Kylie?"

"She's okay. I sat with her while she got checked out by paramedics and made her statement," Kellan said, his eyes shifting around the busy corridor. "But she's tough. And she was definitely adamant about what happened."

"That sounds like her," Devon said. His stomach suddenly felt like someone had dropped it in the spin cycle, but the words had to come out. "Listen, about your sister—"

"Is this the part where you tell me you dig her?"

What. The. Fuck. "Uh," Devon stammered, and seriously, this was not how he'd pictured this going.

Kellan crossed his arms, but the corners of his lips tugged upward into a smile. "Look, I'm not ever going to be wild about my sister seeing anyone, but she told me how she feels about you. What you did to keep her safe. If she's going to be with anyone, it should at least be a guy who's good enough for her."

"Are you sure that guy is me?"

"I trusted you with Kylie's safety from the beginning, man. Not because you were close by, but because you're you." Kellan paused, sliding a hand over the dark stubble covering his chin before continuing. "Look, I know you've carried around a lot of guilt over what happened in Afghanistan. But what happened that day wasn't your fault."

"I know. I mean, I do now," Devon said, and damn, it felt good to mean the words.

"Good. Then you also know you're good enough for my sister."

Devon blinked, shaking the hand Kellan had extended in his direction. "Thanks. I promise to treat her right."

"Do yourself a favor," Kellan said, his blue stare sharpening like razor wire. "Just don't ever tell me about it, okay?"

"Copy that." He bit down on his smile. "You headed back to North Carolina?"

Kellan nodded. "Tomorrow. First I've got some shit to hash out with Detective Moreno, namely how she vouched for a team that nearly got you and Kylie killed."

Whoa. Devon wasn't touching the anger in his voice for all the money in the vault. Somehow, he got the impression that the two of them getting back on board with each other would take more than a conversation. "Got it. I guess I'll go find Kylie. Make sure she's okay."

"I just dropped her off at the Hilton, about six blocks from here," Kellan said. "There's a room reserved for you there too."

"Oh. Okay." A room he didn't have to lock down like Leavenworth sounded like a gift right now. "I'll guess I'll be there if you need me."

Devon found the place easily enough, thank you cell phone GPS, and snagged the keys to his room without any trouble. As badly as he wanted to make sure Kylie was okay, he knew Kellan had barely left her an hour ago—probably after a ridiculously extensive room check—and he needed a shower like nobody's business. Slipping his room key in front of the card reader, he pushed open the door, vowing to take the fastest shower known to man, woman, or child…

Kylie was sitting on the bed, wearing nothing but a robe and a smile.

"Hey," she said, looking so pretty that Devon's chest hurt. "I hope it's okay, but I asked for adjoining rooms." She pointed to a door over her shoulder, and he lifted one corner of his mouth at the irony.

"Since it saves me from having to track you down, I'd say adjoining rooms are very okay."

Her smile grew even bigger. "Well, they kept you longer than I expected, but we can have this warmed up if you want."

Only then did Devon see the room service trays covering the side table across from the bed, and he couldn't help it. He laughed.

"Let me guess," he said, moving over to lift one of the silver domes. *Yep.* "Spaghetti and meatballs."

"I would've made it myself, but my resources are a little limited," she said, slipping from the bed to close the space between them.

Devon wrapped his arms around her, knowing without

question that Kylie was where she belonged, and so was he. "I thought maybe we could look for a kitchen in North Carolina. One that needs an owner. Or two."

"You want to move with me to Remington?" she gasped.

"Like you said, I don't have a crystal ball. I don't know what the future holds, but I do know I want to be wherever you are, Kylie. Starting with right here, right now."

She pressed up to kiss him, covering his smile with hers. "That sounds perfect to me. After all, there's no time like the present."

* * * *

Click here to discover more of Liliana Hart's MacKenzie Family.

* * * *

If you enjoyed your sneak peek at Kellan and Isabella in DEEP TROUBLE and want to check out their story, it's coming in September 2016! Make sure to subscribe to Kimberly's newsletter right here for preorder information and to keep up with the debut of the sexy firefighters of Station Seventeen.

Sign up for the 1001 Dark Nights Newsletter
and be entered to win a Tiffany Lock necklace.

There's a contest every quarter!

Discover the Liliana Hart MacKenzie Family Collection

Trouble Maker
A MacKenzie Family Novel
by Liliana Hart

Marnie Whitlock has never known what it's like to be normal. She and her family moved from place to place, hiding from reporters and psychologists, all because of her gift. A curse was more like it. Seeing a victim, feeling his pain as the last of his life ebbed away, and being helpless to save him. It was torture. And then one day it disappeared and she was free. Until those who hunted her for her gift tried to kill her. And then the gift came back with a vengeance.

Beckett Hamilton leads a simple life. His ranch is profitable and a legacy he'll be proud to pass onto his children one day, work fills his time from sunup to sundown, and his romances are short and sweet. He wouldn't have it any other way. And then he runs into quiet and reserved Marnie Whitlock just after she moves to town. She intrigues him like no woman ever has. And she's hiding something. His hope is that she begins to trust him before it's too late.

* * * *

Rush
A MacKenzie Family Novella
by Robin Covington

From Liliana Hart's New York Times bestselling MacKenzie family comes a new story by USA Today bestselling author Robin Covington...

Atticus Rush doesn't really like people. Years in Special Ops and law enforcement showed him the worst of humanity, making his mountain hideaway the ideal place to live. But when his colleagues at MacKenzie Security need him to save the kidnapped young daughter of a U.S. Senator, he'll do it, even if it means working with the woman who broke his heart …his ex-wife.

Lady Olivia Rutledge-Cairn likes to steal things. Raised with a silver spoon and the glass slipper she spent years cultivating a cadre of acquaintances in the highest places. She parlayed her natural gift for theft into a career of locating and illegally retrieving hard-to-find items of value for the ridiculously wealthy. Rush was the one man who tempted her to change her ways…until he caught her and threatened to turn her in.

MacKenzie Security has vowed to save the girl. Olivia can find anything or anyone. Rush can get anyone out. As the clock winds down on the girl's life, can they fight the past, a ruthless madman and their explosive passion to get the job done?

* * * *

Bullet Proof
A MacKenzie Family Novella
by Avery Flynn

"Being one of the good guys is not my thing."

Bianca Sutherland isn't at an exclusive Eyes-Wide-Shut style orgy for the orgasms. She's there because the only clue to her friend's disappearance is a photo of a painting hanging somewhere in Bisu Manor. Determined to find her missing friend when no one else will, she expects trouble when she cons her way into the party—but not in the form of a so-hot-he-turns-your-panties-to-ash former boxer.

Taz Hazard's only concern is looking out for himself and he

has no intention of changing his ways until he finds sexy-as-sin Bianca at the most notorious mansion in Ft. Worth. Now, he's tangled up in a missing person case tied into a powerful new drug about to flood the streets, if they can't find a way to stop it before its too late. Taking on a drug cartel isn't safe, but when passion ignites between them Taz and Bianca discover their hearts aren't bulletproof either.

* * * *

Delta Rescue
A MacKenzie Family Novella
by Cristin Harber

When Luke Brenner takes an off-the-books job on the MacKenzie-Delta joint task force, he has one goal: shut down sex traffickers on his personal hunt for retribution. This operation brings him closer than he's ever been to avenge his first love, who was taken, sold, and likely dead.

Madeleine Mercier is the daughter of an infamous cartel conglomerate. Their family bleeds money, they sell pleasure, they sell people. She knows no other life, sees no escape, except for one. Maddy is the only person who can take down Papa, when every branch of law enforcement in every country, is on her father's payroll.

It's evil. To want to ruin, to murder, her family. But that's what she is. Ruined for a life outside of destroying her father. She can't feel arousal. Has never been kissed. Never felt anything other than disgust for the world that she perpetuates. Until she clashes with a possible mercenary who gives her hope.

The hunter versus the virgin. The predator and his prey. When forced together, can enemies resist the urge to run away or destroy one another?

* * * *

Desire & Ice
A MacKenzie Family Novella
by Christopher Rice

Danny Patterson isn't a teenager anymore. He's the newest and youngest sheriff's deputy in Surrender, Montana. A chance encounter with his former schoolteacher on the eve of the biggest snowstorm to hit Surrender in years shows him that some schoolboy crushes never fade. Sometimes they mature into grown-up desire.

It's been years since Eliza Brightwell set foot in Surrender. So why is she back now? And why does she seem like she's running from something? To solve this mystery, Danny disobeys a direct order from Sheriff Cooper MacKenzie and sets out into a fierce blizzard, where his courage and his desire might be the only things capable of saving Eliza from a dark force out of her own past.

1001 Dark Nights

Welcome to 1001 Dark Nights… a collection of novellas that are breathtakingly sexy and magically romantic. Some are paranormal, some are erotic. Each and every one is compelling and page turning.

Inspired by the exotic tales of The Arabian Nights, 1001 Dark Nights features *New York Times* and *USA Today* bestselling authors.

In the original, Scheherazade desperately attempts to entertain her husband, the King of Persia, with nightly stories so that he will postpone her execution.

In our versions, month after month, each of our fabulous authors puts a unique spin on the premise and creates a tale that a new Scheherazade tells long into the dark, dark night.

For more information, visit www.1001DarkNights.com

About Kimberly Kincaid

Kimberly Kincaid writes contemporary romance novels that split the difference between sexy and sweet. When she's not sitting cross-legged in an ancient desk chair known as "The Pleather Bomber", she can be found practicing obscene amounts of yoga, whipping up anything from enchiladas to eclairs in her kitchen, or curled up with her nose in a book. Kimberly is a *USA Today* best-selling author and a 2015 RWA RITA finalist who lives (and writes!) by the mantra that food is love. She is the author of over a dozen books, and she resides in Virginia with her wildly patient husband and their three daughters.

Want the scoop on the sizzling heroes and sassy heroines of Station Seventeen, plus the chance to win five free books every month? Sign up for Kimberly Kincaid's newsletter, and check out these other sexy titles, available at your favorite retailers!

And for hot news and even hotter Man Candy, don't forget to come find Kimberly on Facebook, join her street team The Taste Testers, and follow her on Twitter and Pinterest!

On behalf of 1001 Dark Nights,

Liz Berry and M.J. Rose would like to thank ~

Liliana Hart
Scott Silverii
Steve Berry
Doug Scofield
Kim Guidroz
Jillian Stein
InkSlinger PR
Asha Hossain
Kasi Alexander
Chris Graham
Pamela Jamison
Jessica Johns
Dylan Stockton
and Simon Lipskar

Made in the USA
Columbia, SC
26 June 2017